PENGUIN BOOKS

ANNIE BESANT

Rosemary Dinnage has worked in publishing, translating, and research psychology. She is now a freelance journalist and contributes to several literary journals in Britain and the United States.

LIVES OF MODERN WOMEN

General Editor: Emma Tennant

Lives of Modern Women is a series of short biographical portraits by distinguished writers of women whose ideas, struggles and creative talents have made a significant contribution to the way we think and live now.

It is hoped that both the fascination of comparing the aims, ideals, setbacks and achievements of those who confronted and contributed to a world in transition and the high quality of writing and insight will encourage the reader to delve further into the lives and work of some of this country's most extraordinary and necessary women.

Rosemary Dinnage

Annie Besant

Penguin Books

Penguin Books Ltd, Harmondsworth, Middlesex, England
Viking Penguin Inc., 40 West 23rd Street, New York, New York 10010, U.S.A.
Penguin Books Australia Ltd, Ringwood, Victoria, Australia
Penguin Books Canada Limited, 2801 John Street, Markham, Ontario, Canada L3R 1B4
Penguin Books (N.Z.) Ltd, 182–190 Wairau Road, Auckland 10, New Zealand

First published 1986

Made and printed in Great Britain by
Richard Clay Ltd, Bungay, Suffolk
Filmset in Monophoto Photina

CONTENTS

LIST OF PLATES

Annie Wood at sixteen (courtesy of Dr Hugh Gray, General
Secretary, The Theosophical Society in England)
Annie Wood with her mother (courtesy of Dr Hugh Gray, General
Secretary, The Theosophical Society in England)
Annie Besant (BBC Hulton Picture Library)
Charles Bradlaugh (BBC Hulton Picture Library)
A card for a Fabian lecture, 1886 (reproduced from *The First Five
Lives of Annie Besant*, 1961)
Members of the match girls' union, 1888 (BBC Hulton Picture
Library)
Madame Helena Petrovna Blavatsky (courtesy of Dr Hugh
Gray, General Secretary, The Theosophical Society in
England)
Caricature by Phil May (BBC Hulton Picture Library)
Krishnamurti in 1911 (courtesy of Dr Hugh Gray, General
Secretary, The Theosophical Society in England)
A group of leading Theosophists including Annie Besant, C. W.
Leadbeater, Krishnamurti, Nitya (courtesy of Dr Hugh Gray,
General Secretary, The Theosophical Society in England)
Annie Besant with daughter Mabel and grandchild (courtesy of Dr
Hugh Gray, General Secretary, The Theosophical Society in
England)
Annie at the Queen's Hall (courtesy of Dr Hugh Gray, General
Secretary, The Theosophical Society in England)

LIST OF PLATES

1847   Birth of Annie Wood in London.

1855   Annie leaves home to be educated by Ellen Marryat, returning eight years later.

1867   Marriage to Frank Besant, a clergyman.

1869   Son Digby born.

1871   Daughter Mabel born.

1873   Annie loses her faith and leaves her husband, taking Mabel with her.

1874   Annie meets Charles Bradlaugh, a crusading atheist, and starts lecturing and writing for the National Secular Society.

1877   The 'Knowlton trial': prosecution of Annie Besant and Charles Bradlaugh for publishing a book on contraception.

1879   After a year of legal battles, Frank Besant gains permanent custody of Mabel as well as Digby on the grounds that Annie is unfit to bring her up.
        Annie studies for a degree in science.

1885   She espouses socialism and joins the Fabian Society, writing, travelling and lecturing for them.

1887   'Bloody Sunday'.

1888   Annie leads the strike of girls working at Bryant and May's factory.

	She is elected to the London School Board.
1889	Meeting with Madame Blavatsky and conversion to Theosophy.
1891	Madame Blavatsky dies and Annie becomes leader of the Theosophical Society in Europe and India.
1893	First visit to India, which becomes her home.
1898	Founds the first of several schools in India.
1907	Becomes President of the Theosophical Society.
1909	Krishnamurti, aged fourteen, is chosen to be the new World Teacher.
1913	Starts political work for India.
1914	Annie wins the guardianship of Krishnamurti. Launches the *Commonweal* and the *New India*.
1917	Internment in Ootacamund. President of India's National Congress.
1919	Massacre at Amritsar. Gandhi eclipses Annie in India.
1929	Krishnamurti dissociates himself from his role and the Theosophical Society.
1933	Death of Annie Besant.

CHAPTER ONE

Annie Besant wrote her autobiography – up to the age of forty-four, about half of her long life – twice over. In the first version she wrote, with conventional decorum, that it was in 1847 that she made her appearance 'in this "vale of tears"'; in the second, written after she became a Theosophist, she started with her horoscope and a digression on the value of astrology. This second version was prefaced with a declaration that since her conversion to Theosophy, 'never once, for a single instant, has my faith in it faltered, nor the slightest cloud of distrust flitted across my sky'; life after Theosophy was no longer a vale of tears. We have to believe her.

Can we call Annie Besant a 'modern' woman? She was a phenomenon; a pioneer of pioneers. Yet in many ways she remained a product of the Victorian age into which she was born. The Victorians, so near to us in time, often seem extraordinary to us, and there can hardly have been a more extraordinary example of the breed than Annie Besant. At sixteen, she was a passionate Christian who flagellated herself and begged Christ in her prayers to 'let him kiss me with the kisses of His mouth; for Thy love is better than wine'. At twenty-eight, she was notorious as a leader of militant atheism, and was to have her children forcibly removed from her because of her pernicious influence. At thirty, she was publicly tried at law for publishing an 'obscene' pamphlet outlining methods of birth control. At thirty-six, she was converted to socialism; she fought the police on 'Bloody Sunday' in Trafalgar Square, and she went out in support of a strike of women workers. At forty-one, as a member of the powerful London School Board, she introduced free lunches and medical treatment for the first time in elementary schools. At forty-two, she was converted for life to a 'religion' hastily patched together by a psychic Russian aristocrat on the basis of occult messages from Tibetan gurus in the Himalayas. At sixty-six, after many years in India spreading the Theosophical gospel, she took up the cause of Indian independence and later presided over the Indian National Congress in Calcutta.

Annie Besant will not fit neatly into a feminist, revolutionary image to please the twentieth century. Her commitment to social betterment was certainly a cornerstone of her character, but there was also the nineteenth-century strain of profound religiosity. Those who have written about her have tried hard to find a key to the extraordinary variety of causes to which she committed herself during her lifetime. Bernard Shaw, a close friend and colleague at one time, unkindly claimed that what she really wanted was to act out a succession of dramatic roles. One of her biographers finds the key in a martyr complex; and indeed she says herself that from girlhood on she saw herself as leading, and suffering for, some great cause. *Leading*, not following. She had a powerful will and was a born organizer; above all, her energy and courage were of an extraordinary order.

But, as she wrote herself, 'if any one would understand

the evolution of a Soul he must be willing to face the questions which the Soul faces in its growth'. The religious search was the thread that ran most consistently through her extraordinarily varied career. One may be misled by her fourteen years as one of the leaders of Freethought, as the anti-Church atheistic movement was called. Freethought itself was a kind of militant religion ('if "morality touched by emotion" be religion, then truly I was the most religious of Atheists'), as was socialism; she was never, in the twentieth-century fashion, *non*-religious. In her movement from one crusading passion to another there was a consistency. And all her faiths were linked by a concern for social betterment – she was never for a cloistered, apolitical faith.

The religious influences on her childhood were significantly mixed. Annie Wood was three-quarters Irish, the middle child of an Irish mother and a half-Irish father, though she was born and grew up in England. William Wood worked in the City, but he was a scholar and dilettante, interested in medicine, master of classical and modern languages, devoted to literature – and, though he came of a Catholic family, a religious sceptic. His wife was Protestant, and sufficiently influenced by her husband to have discarded such doctrines as eternal punishment and biblical infallibility. She liked a pretty service, an attractive church – 'dainty and well-bred piety', her daughter was to call it. None of Annie's religions were to be dainty and well-bred. Her mother, on the other hand, bemoaned the fact that her daughter 'had always been too religious'.

Disaster struck the family when Annie was five. In her autobiography she relates the tragedy in full-blown Victorian fashion: William Wood, following his medical interests, attended the post-mortem of a man who had died of tuberculosis, and scratched his finger on the breastbone. The cut would not heal, and was followed by his catching cold; the doctor predicted a galloping consumption, and indeed within three months William Wood was dead. Annie, clutching her doll, was taken in to 'say goodbye to papa'. Mrs Wood then shut herself in her room overnight; and next morning emerged with snow-white hair! Annie Besant was a woman of integrity, but she was to write and believe many very extraordinary things. Was the snow-white hair an early example of her ability to believe what her imagination dictated to her?

Wood left no money, and his widow moved to Harrow so that she could take in boy boarders and send her son to public school (the other boy had died not long after his father). Here Annie remembered being very happy, climbing into her favourite trees to read *Pilgrim's Progress* and *Paradise Lost* – books, of course, of religious heroism. 'How much easier to be a Christian if one could have a red-cross shield and a white banner, and a beautiful Divine Prince to smile at you when the battle was over.' When she was eight her life changed drastically. A philanthropic spinster lady, Miss Ellen Marryat, took a fancy to Annie Wood and offered to bring her up. Miss Marryat was already caring for two children from large and impecunious families, and she offered to educate Annie in term-time and send her home for the holidays. So Annie was carried off to Miss Marryat's country estate in Dorset.

Certainly this turn of events led to Annie having a genuine education, rather than that of a Victorian young lady; Ellen Marryat was an unconventional and gifted teacher (the boys even learned to sew on their own buttons). There was no rote-learning, as in most schools of the time; instead of poring over spelling-books and grammars, the children learned to write, in lucid style, their own compositions on what interested them. They were taught to think clearly and to think for themselves. Annie was to owe much to this education.

On the other hand she was young to leave her adored mother, and perhaps acquired from the separation a strain of solemnity that she was to combat with hard work all her life. And she was subjected now to a third religious attitude, different both from her father's and her mother's. Miss Marryat was an extreme evangelical; sin, damnation, conversion, and permanent recourse to the Scriptures formed the regime. Perhaps the first seed of Annie's career as an orator was planted here. The children were called on for extemporary prayer, 'speaking to the Lord', and, in spite of shyness, she felt she did it rather well. On Sundays only the Bible and the lives of the martyrs were permitted reading, encouraging more daydreams of facing the stake or the rack.

When Annie was sixteen Miss Marryat and 'family' went to the Continent to get treatment for one of the boys. In Germany Annie's mind was healthily distracted from religion for a time while she was pursued by ardent German youths. In Paris, however, what impressed her most were the churches. She discovered the sensuous enjoyment of colour and fragrance and pomp in church services, and a fourth strand was added to her religious education. In Paris she was confirmed, and, never having been to a theatre or a ball, was ardent to renounce both as representatives of the world, the flesh and the devil ('little prig that I was'). She was not allowed to read love-stories, and 'as my girlhood began to bud towards womanhood, all its deeper currents set in the direction of religious devotion'. She wanted to be a saint, a martyr, a prophetess.

University was, of course, not to be thought of for a girl in the 1860s. That was for brothers; it is curious that Annie Besant, devoted to her mother, scarcely refers to her brother in her autobiography. It is a reasonable guess that she felt competitive towards him and his opportunities. At this time she was reading German literature in the original, Plato in translation, Dante, the English Romantics, the *Faerie Queen*, and, above all, theology: Augustine, Chrysostom, Barnabas, Ignatius, Clement, Origen – and the fashionable moderns, Keble and Pusey. She fasted, flagellated and prayed. Life was not quite all religion, though; she was accomplished on the piano beyond the average young lady, she rode and played croquet and archery, she even – now that she had left Ellen Marryat and come home – went to balls. But she had been allowed to know little of novels or plays, and in her thoughts she still conquered Heaven rather than young men.

It was not surprising, then, that she found herself, half unawares, hustled into an engagement at eighteen with a shy and austere young clergyman. As she tells the story, she was so aghast at his hasty proposal that she could not collect her wits to say no. And then wives of clergymen had such opportunities for self-sacrifice: watching at sickbeds, knitting for the cottager's child, cheering the old and taking nutritious soups to the hungry. For a girl passionate to do good and achieve something, being a clergyman's wife offered almost a career when no other was available. 'All that was deepest and truest in my nature,' she wrote, 'chafed against my easy, useless days, longed for work, yearned to devote itself, as I had read women saints had done, to the battling against sin and misery.' And on to many a prosaic

English clergyman the halo of the saints and martyrs shed a faint reflected glow for their prospective brides. 'She could not be the bride of Heaven, and therefore became the wife of Mr Frank Besant,' said her friend W. T. Stead, the editor, later. 'He was hardly an adequate substitute.'

Around the time of her engagement there were two events which foreshadowed later developments in her life. In Holy Week of that year she set out to write a brief devotional history of the events of the week, compiled from the four gospels. She set out each narrative in a separate column, and to her horror found that the accounts of each day from Palm Sunday to Good Friday did not tally. It is hard now to imagine the frame of mind where discrepancies in historical accounts written long after the event should shake a faith to its foundations, but so it was. Firmly she repeated to herself Tertullian's *'Credo quia impossibile'* (a phrase that was to do good service later in her life). But it was the first seed of doubt. 'I smothered it up, buried it, and smoothed the turf over its grave'; and she wrote an essay on the duty of fasting, which she presented to her fiancé.

At this same time her political and social conscience was beginning to be aroused. She went to stay with friends in Manchester and became something of a pet of the elderly husband, William Roberts. 'Lawyer Roberts' was much loved by the workers of Manchester for his unpaid work on their behalf. For Annie, up to that time, the poor were unfortunates who were to be charitably looked after; Roberts taught her fiercely that they were the wealth-producers of the country, entitled not to charity but to justice. She left behind the 'decorous Whiggism' that for eighteen years she had absorbed through her pores.

While she was still in Manchester she witnessed a *cause*

célèbre that she never forgot. Three young Fenian protesters from Ireland were hanged outside Salford Gaol for their resistance to the police. Annie Wood saw the judges' black caps being got ready in a back room and heard the condemned men shout: 'God save Ireland!' after the sentence. As an old woman in India she wrote that the love of liberty was first sparked in her when she heard that death sentence pronounced and the following shout of 'God save Ireland!'

These were not, perhaps, good omens for life as a country clergyman's wife. In December 1867, Annie 'sailed out of the safe harbour of my happy and peaceful girlhood on to the wide sea of life, and the waves broke roughly as soon as the bar was crossed'. They were soon to be very rough indeed.

CHAPTER TWO

The unpromising marriage seems to have been doomed from the start. Annie Besant makes it clear in her autobiography that sexual shock was one of the factors in its doom; like so many Victorian girls, she entered marriage the personification of ignorance and chastity. But so did other girls, and their marriages seldom ended in separation within a few years. Frank Besant seems to have been rigid, charmless and entirely set in his belief that a husband's word is law within his household; Annie was delicate and intellectual and cosseted. She had never, she claims, heard a harsh word spoken to her, and 'never had a worry touched me' (not a likely story, for someone of twenty). It is curious that, believing marriage to be the one and only destiny of women, Victorian families so often sent their daughters into it not only sexually ignorant but ignorant of housekeeping and money management; Victorian novels, though, attest to it. The young bride struggles with Cook and the housekeeping bills, pines for her mother, and cries in secret.

Writing in middle life, Annie Besant generously doubts that she was ever cut out to be an ordinary wife; not only had she been shielded from all practical matters, but under her delicate exterior there was, as she says, 'a woman of strong dominant will, strength that panted for expression and rebelled under restraint'. The Reverend Frank Besant must have been as stunned by the shock of marriage as she was. For her, shock turned to distress and distress to cold bitterness. Fortunately she had her books. She was infinitely bored by talk of recipes and sewing patterns and whether Cook should have used lard instead of butter.

She was also taking, around this time, her first steps in what was to be an unstoppable writing career. She sent off some stories to the *Family Herald* and for a few guineas they were accepted. One of them – 'Sunshine and Shade: A Tale founded on Fact' – tells of a young wife who, after two months of marriage, has an accident and is paralysed. Was it founded on fact in the sense that she felt marriage had paralysed her? She was immensely pleased to have earned money of her own for the first time in her life. She realized very soon that it was not indeed her own; unless legally protected, every penny a married woman had belonged to her husband.

Her first child, Digby, was born in 1869, and eighteen months later her daughter Mabel. When Mabel was a few months old she fell desperately ill of whooping-cough. Annie nursed her night and day in a steam tent and after the gravest danger the child began to recover. Annie collapsed with the strain herself, and from the time of this illness another and even more desperate struggle began. The learned, pious young vicar's wife began to lose her faith.

Her marriage had initiated her into a new world of harshness and pain. Her own feelings had been grossly insulted, and she had seen her child suffer wretchedly. She had, besides, been visiting the poor as part of her parochial duties and had learned how the mass of the people were forced to live. Her logical mind, never satisfied with easy answers, began to question how a benevolent God could allow such things.

One cannot underestimate what the loss of religious faith meant in Annie Besant's time. For her it was to involve a revolution in her life, but for *any* earnest Victorian it was a cataclysm. She was not exaggerating when she wrote that

there is in life no other pain so horrible, so keen in its torture, so crushing in its weight. It seems to shipwreck everything, to destroy the one steady gleam of happiness 'on the other side' that no earthly storm could obscure . . . No life in the empty sky; no gleam in the blackness of the night; no voice to break the deadly silence; no hand outstretched to save.

The process was slow, orderly and excruciating, and lasted for more than three years from start to finish. At one point she considered suicide. As religious doubt settled firmly over her, she decided to divide the structure of Christianity into separate points and test out each one in turn. Each crumbled under her scrutiny, but the sum of her questions was familiar: if God was good, how could he allow evil? If he allowed evil, how could he be omnipotent? She read endlessly, and none of the books answered her. The country clergyman's wife boldly made an appointment to put her doubts to the theologian Edward Pusey in Oxford. Pusey thundered at her that she was blaspheming, that he forbade her to spread the infection of disbelief to another soul. 'It is not your duty to ascertain the truth,' he said. But this was something she was never to believe.

Annie left the eminent man battered but steadfast. For a time on her progress she found a resting-place among the Theists, who accepted a God without the Christian trappings. For her Theism 'was free from the defects which revolted me in Christianity . . . dreams of ignorant and semi-savage minds, not the revelation of a God'. She began to write pamphlets, the first on 'The Deity of Jesus of Nazareth'. For the Christian trappings she had dispensed with included the divinity of Christ; and now the question arose of whether her conscience could let her go through the ceremony of taking Holy Communion. Logical and uncompromising, one day Annie stood up in church when the Communion was ready and, feeling everyone's eyes on her, walked out. The villagers took it for granted that she had been taken ill, and further explanations hardly penetrated their rustic minds.

It was at this time that she undertook a curious experiment, one with great implications for her future. She had come into the church to practise the organ. She locked the church doors, climbed into the pulpit, and delivered a sermon to the empty pews – curiously enough, on the inspiration of the Bible rather than on something more heretical and atheistic. She enjoyed it tremendously; she found her voice confident and musical, her cadences rhythmical, her inspiration flowing freely. It was that first feeling of *power*, she wrote in her autobiography, that she would never forget. Perhaps she had just wanted to prove that she could preach a better sermon than Frank Besant, but she had discovered a gift that was going to be central to her life. Whatever her sufferings over the slow loss of her faith, she was also gaining from it a voice and a will.

In 1873, when she was twenty-five years old, the inevitable happened and her marriage broke up. She was presented with the choice – attend Communion, or leave; and she left. It was a drastic and terrifying step for a young wife to take at that time.

She was less unlucky than some women might have been in her position. Possessing no money of her own, a wife had little power to take legal action against a husband, and by leaving the home she lost jurisdiction over her children. Possibly she cited evidence of actual cruelty from Frank Besant. At any rate, a legal separation was agreed and she was allowed to keep Mabel and a tiny sum of money, leaving Digby with his father. Whatever she felt about leaving her first-born, she says nothing about it in her autobiography. She quitted the vicarage, and went out to work as house-keeper/governess in return for board and lodging for herself and Mabel. But her cherished plan was to set up house with her mother. Now a new blow fell. Her mother was taken seriously ill, and after nursing her for a time Annie realized that she was not going to live. With the approach of death another religious crisis loomed. Mrs Wood, dying, would not take the Sacrament unless Annie took it with her: 'I would rather be lost with Annie than saved without her.' Annie eventually found an ultra-liberal clergyman who allowed that Annie in her disbelief could take the Sacrament without sinning, and the thing was done. Mrs Wood died at peace. Annie was bereft.

The next two months, Annie Besant writes in her auto-biography, were the worst of her life. The fact that she had been separated from her mother for so much of her childhood had only intensified her feeling for her. Now she was without her son and her mother and as yet without any means of support. She earned a little money by writing Theist tracts, but she often went hungry.

In her progress from ecstatic piety to atheism she had only a few more steps to go. She was reading Comte and Mill, attending the South Place Chapel – ultra-rationalist but not quite Freethought or atheism – and writing tracts for Thomas Scott, a Freethought leader. Eventually she proposed to Scott that she should write one on the question of the existence of God. 'Ah, little lady, you are facing, then, that problem at last?' said Scott. 'I thought it must come. Write away.' Her essay proposed that 'we can no longer mean by [God] a personal being in the orthodox sense, possessing an individuality which divides him from the rest of the universe'. When she came to join the National Secular Society she first asked earnestly whether it was necessary actually to 'profess Atheism' before joining – it was the point she had not yet quite reached. The last step would be taken when she met Charles Bradlaugh.

To be a non-Christian in the late nineteenth century was not a simple matter of slipping out of the Church – not for everyone, anyway. The Church remained so powerful that a comparable structure of opposition was organized against it. Freethought was run rather like a religion; it had its Freethought halls, its Sunday meetings, its secular sermons, its weekly journals and its publishing press – there was even to be a Secular Hymn Book.

At the head of the movement stood Charles Bradlaugh. Son of a nursemaid and a clerk, he left school at eleven but soon started a career as a young prodigy of a speaker on Freethought and temperance. He went into the army for three years, and when he came out became a solicitor's errand-boy, then his clerk, meanwhile teaching himself law. He had travelled to Italy in support of Mazzini and Garibaldi, and had been lionized in the United States.

Bradlaugh had continually to do battle against legal disputes and debts, yet he had built up the National Secular Society as a nationwide organization and ran his own newspaper, the *National Reformer*. He was a storm-centre for both devotion and hatred from the public. Bernard Shaw wrote of him that 'he was quite simply a hero; a single champion of anti-Christendom against the seventy-seven champions of Christendom. He was not a leader: he was a wonder whom men followed and obeyed. He was a terrific opponent, making his way by an overwhelming personal force which reduced his most formidable rivals to pigmies.' In particular he was renowned for his oratory on the platform; when a friend recommended to Annie that she should go to hear him, she described him as the finest speaker she knew – 'His power over a crowd is something marvellous. Whether you agree with him or not, you should hear him.' Certainly Annie must go.

Her membership of the National Secular Society was accepted in spite of the fact that she did not – quite yet – 'profess Atheism', and in the summer of 1874 she went to Bradlaugh's headquarters, the Hall of Science, as a new member. It was her first visit to a Freethought hall.

The hall was crowded to suffocation, and, at the very moment announced for the lecture, a roar of cheering burst forth, a tall figure passed swiftly up the Hall to the platform, and, with a slight bow in answer to the voluminous greeting, Charles Bradlaugh took his seat. I looked at him with interest, impressed and surprised. The grave, quiet, stern, strong face, the massive head, the keen eyes, the magnificent breadth and height of forehead – was this the man I had heard described as a blatant agitator, an ignorant demagogue? . . . The great audience, carried away by the torrent of the orator's force, hung silent, breathing soft, as he went on, till the silence that followed a magnificent peroration broke the spell, and a hurricane of cheers relieved the tension.

Curiously, in view of Annie Besant's future, Bradlaugh's topic that evening was a comparison of the myths of Krishna and of Christ. Afterwards he came up and spoke to her; clearly they must have been a handsome pair, Bradlaugh broad and tall and Annie, at that time, slender, pretty, and fond of dressing in neat dark dresses with a touch of white. He invited her to visit him at his lodgings to discuss their beliefs, and when she did so she took with her her paper on the existence of God. From their talk she came away knowing she was an atheist – 'You have thought yourself into Atheism without knowing it,' said Bradlaugh.

Later, writing her autobiography as a convinced Theosophist, Annie Besant translated their instant mutual sympathy into the terms of her new creed, it was not just liking at first sight, it was a question of reincarnation; they must have met in other lives. And in spite of the estrangement that took place later in their lives, she wrote there with the greatest warmth of a friendship that 'lasted unbroken till Death severed the earthly bond'. She owed him, she says, more than she could express in terms of advice, support and encouragement – and he was a stern critic as well:

It will be a good thing for the world when a friendship between a man and a woman no longer means a protective condescension on one side and helpless dependence on the other, but when they meet on equal ground of intellectual sympathy, discussing, criticizing, studying, and so aiding the evolution of stronger and clearer thought-ability in each.

'What of value there is in my work,' she believed, 'is very largely due to his influence.' This was a generous exaggeration. Bradlaugh himself quickly recognized the calibre of his new acquaintance, for straight away he offered her a job on the *National Reformer* as columnist and reviewer. The salary was one guinea a week – very welcome to the almost penniless Annie. Within three weeks of joining the National Secular Society she was writing her first column for the paper under the pen-name of 'Ajax', having stepped over the last thin line that divided her from atheism. She wrote about bishops and spiritualism – both, she declared, equally ridiculous – and cremation and secular education, and about international news of the atheist cause. Within the next few weeks she had written with equal facility on science, economics, literature and agricultural reform. Bradlaugh had discovered his invaluable ally.

Their personal friendship proceeded just as quickly. After their first discussion of atheism in Bradlaugh's study, Annie invited him to visit. He reminded her that he had a scandalous reputation, but she proudly reiterated the invitation. In fact in terms of personal morality Bradlaugh was impeccably careful; the professed atheist must be like Caesar's wife, he believed. His marriage, like Annie's, was effectively over; he had married a pretty and cheerful girl with a fatal fondness for drink. Very soon, his daughter wrote in her biography of him,

this weakness developed into absolute and confirmed intemperance, which it seemed as though nothing could check ... Easy goodnature became extravagant folly, and was soon followed by the alienation of real friends and a ruined home. My father was gentleness and forbearance itself, but his life was utterly poisoned.

Eventually he separated from her, and his daughters spent much of their time with him in his cramped lodgings. His wife died a few years after he met Annie Besant, but Frank

Besant was not so obliging. The two were never free to marry, but it was assumed by those who knew them that otherwise they would have done.

In one of her Freethought pamphlets Annie Besant compares the Christian ideal of the Man of Sorrows with the new ideal of the atheist:

In form strong and fair, perfect in physical development as the Hercules of Grecian art, radiant with love, glorious in self-reliant power; with lips bent firm to resist oppression, and melting into soft curves of passion and of pity; with deep, far-seeing eyes, gazing piercingly into the secrets of the unknown, and resting lovingly on the beauties around him; with hands strong to work in the present; with heart full of hope which the future shall realize; making earth glad with his labour and beautiful with his skill — this, this is the Ideal Man, enshrined in the Atheist's heart.

The prose was, for her, a little overheated, for she was always a competent writer. Was she dreaming of Charles Bradlaugh as the atheist ideal, the 'beautiful Divine Prince to smile at you when the battle was over'?

CHAPTER THREE

Within the space of a very few years Annie Besant had come a long way. She had experienced marital misery for the first time, borne children and seen them suffer, undergone a stubborn and painful intellectual change of heart, set out for the first time to live as a woman alone, been hungry and poor, and lost her son and her mother. Though she had a few loyal friends, she was already outside the conventions of the society of her time and very much alone. Her trials had strengthened but not hardened her; nevertheless she was still shy, uncertain of what her future could possibly be and to what she should commit herself. In meeting Bradlaugh and taking the decisive step of joining the Freethought cause with him she had begun to tap the reserves of energy, passion and skill that had so far had no outlet. She had found somewhere she belonged and something she wanted to do – and someone ideally fitted to teach and encourage her.

Her career as a speaker was about to start. After a couple of informal practice runs, she gave her first public lecture. It was on 'The Political Status of Women', and it was a success, printed later as a pamphlet. Before the lecture she was terrified, but once on the platform she felt full of power and confidence. It was always to be like this, throughout her speaking career. Her name now went down on a regular list of lecturers, billed to speak not only in London but around the country. At the turn of the years 1874/5 she had made the definite decision to make Freethought her life's work, to go out and speak and write for it.

The desire to spread liberty and truer thought among men, to war against bigotry and superstition, to make the world freer and better than I found it – all this impelled me with a force that would not be denied. I seemed to hear the voice of Truth ringing over the battle-field: 'Who will go? Who will speak for me?' And I sprang forward with passionate enthusiasm, with resolute cry: 'Here am I, send me!'

Annie had always had 'delicate lungs', and before she started on public work she went to ask her doctor whether a public career would harm her. 'It will be kill or cure,' the doctor told her; and a cure it was. A cure for what might otherwise have been her fate as one of the many frustrated, semi-invalid, beshawled Victorian ladies who were – delicate.

Within a matter of months she had started out quite alone on a barnstorming lecture tour of the provinces (her great-aunt meanwhile acting as governess to Mabel). She was booed and hissed and clapped and cheered in equal proportions. She was becoming known; soon indeed she was to be notorious. When her *nom-de-plume* 'Ajax' was discarded, her brother-in-law Walter Besant tried hard to get the newspapers to suppress her real name, but failed. The provincial tour over, she spoke for the first time at the Hall of Science, on 'The God of Christianity versus the God of Freethought'. The hall was packed, and she was cheered vociferously.

Soon she was off again travelling the country, sometimes speaking with Bradlaugh, sometimes on her own. An enthusiast has written of the impression she made at this time:

She still seems incomparably young and attractive, her face alive with emotion and expression, her voice full and sonorous, but musical and not unfeminine. She was perhaps too uniformly earnest and indignant in her denunciation of bigotry and obscurantism, rarely indulging in wit. She was, or we thought she was, a martyr; she had won freedom from domestic and clerical oppression at the cost of social proscription. She faced a hostile world on behalf of liberty and truth. We young men, who had the passion of these things in our souls, responded readily to the passion with which she pleaded for them. We were carried away. Mrs Besant's portrait was for sale at the close of the lecture and I still have the copy which I bought at the time. Its colours are now faded, but the image of this young prophetess of religious and political progress as she appeared on her first lecturing tour is still fresh in my mind.

To the general public, though, she was anathema. In spite of her views on women's rights, the women's suffrage movement did not dare accept her, a militant anti-Christian, among their ranks.

For the next couple of years the writing and lecturing circuit were to continue. Sometimes she travelled in farm carts, fought off drunks, slept in miners' cottages, was stoned and kicked and spat at. In 1875, still a relative newcomer, she was made a vice-president at the National Secular Society's convention. Her lecture list lengthened and converts to Freethought increased.

The atheism to which she now dedicated her life was a serious faith indeed. In her autobiography, writing as a Theosophist and anxious to defend her younger self, she devotes a whole chapter to 'Atheism as I Knew It and Taught

It'. A basic assumption – and this was in the essay on God's possible existence which she wrote before meeting Bradlaugh – was a oneness of matter and spirit: 'there can be only one eternal and underived substance, and matter and spirit must, therefore, only be varying manifestations of this one substance'. This monist universe she assumed to be eternal and evolving, though no personal 'being' called God could exist apart from it. And it was perhaps of divine substance in itself – here 'we have reached a region into which we cannot penetrate; here all human faculties fail us; we bow our heads on "the threshold of the unknown"'. Her brand of atheism, as it now developed in step with Bradlaugh's, was what we would now prefer to call agnosticism; it asserted that the word 'God' had no discernible meaning But Annie Besant was always emotional rather than philosophic, and in a burst of indignant feeling her exposition reverts to the old grievance against pain:

My heart revolts against the spectre of an Almighty Indifference to the pain of sentient beings. My conscience rebels against the injustice, the cruelty, the inequality, which surround me on every side. But I believe in Man. In man's redeeming power; in man's remoulding energy; in man's approaching triumph through knowledge, love, and work.

All the godlike attributes that had been drained out of the Christian divinity were transferred to Man, to the new, perfectible man who was going forward to transform the world. It was a religion of progress, entirely of its time in its optimism. Individuals were not eternal – 'life and death are two convenient words for expressing the general outcome of two arrangements of matter' – but the material universe was, and every being in it had meaning and the potentiality for bettering it. Without the support of a God, morality assumed an even greater importance than it did within Christianity, for there was no one to command or forgive. Doing good to please God was far inferior to doing good for the sake of one's fellows. 'What is your heaven? A heaven in the clouds! I point to a heaven attainable on earth.'

The atheist, clearly, had much to live up to. To those who argued that human nature was flawed and in need of redemption, Annie Besant offered only magnificent scorn – 'if, like silly children, you learn your lesson not to gain knowledge but to win sugar-plums, then you had better go back to your creeds and your churches'. Science taught that man had already evolved from base origins, and, splendidly, he would go on. Evil was no longer something bafflingly sanctioned by God but something to fight and conquer. The perfecting of the race, of the very universe, offered enough challenge and high-mindedness and sacrifice even to Annie Besant.

Atheist is one of the grandest titles a man can wear; it is the Order of Merit of the world's heroes. Most great discoverers, most deep-thinking philosophers, most earnest reformers, most toiling pioneers of progress, have in their turn had flung at them the name of Atheist. It was howled over the grave of Copernicus; it was clamoured round the death-pile of Bruno; it was yelled at Vanini, at Spinoza, at Priestley, at Voltaire, at Paine; it has become the laurel-bay of the hero, the halo of the martyr; in the world's history it has meant the pioneer of progress, and where the cry of 'Atheist' is raised there may we be sure that another step is being taken towards the redemption of humanity.

Audiences cheered, booed, wept, adored; and Annie travelled indefatigably on, spreading her gospel.

Slight and 'delicate' in the lungs she may have been, but clearly one of the keys to Annie Besant's character was that she thrived on work as few people do. Later in her life, when she was deprived of it for a time, she almost collapsed. Bradlaugh's daughter Hypatia wrote: 'Tireless as a worker, she could both write and study longer without rest and respite than any other person I have known; and such was her power of concentration that she could work under circumstances which would have confounded almost every other person.'

Throughout 1875 and 1876, as well as her lecturing she was writing for three periodicals, including a column and several book reviews each week; involving herself in agitation for agricultural reform, and organizing her 'Monster Petition'. This was directed against the granting of huge sums to the royal family – in particular the sum of £142,000 to the Prince of Wales for a projected trip to India, viewed by Besant and Bradlaugh as disguised imperialist propaganda. By the summer of 1876 the strip of signatures was almost a mile long; it was rolled around a pole and driven with great ceremony to the House of Commons, headed 'The petition of the undersigned Charles Bradlaugh, Annie Besant, Charles Watts, and 102,934 others'. The publicity was good; the tour unfortunately went ahead.

Annie Besant's interest in agricultural reform dated from her days working among the poor as a clergyman's wife. Though she was not – as yet – a proclaimed socialist, at no time since girlhood had she been unaware of the depths of poverty in prosperous Victorian Britain. She travelled with Bradlaugh to Yorkshire to make a speech to striking miners, and she attended her first demonstration. At the same time she was dealing with squabbles at the Hall of Science; Bradlaugh was taken seriously ill while away in the United States, and it was left to her to conciliate jealousies. She even wrote a new rallying-cry for members, the 'English Marseillaise', and sang it to great applause at the Hall. The song had a long and successful career in Freethought circles.

It was in 1875 that Frank Besant made his first attempt to kidnap Mabel from her mother. Under the terms of the separation agreement the little girl spent a holiday with her father every year. This time he found that she had forgotten all her prayers – worse, she reported that she had been told not to say them because there was no God to hear them. Frank Besant was outraged and wrote to his legal advisers about taking over custody of Mabel. Bradlaugh and Annie went down together to the vicarage and were turned away with the story that she was not there. Annie threatened court proceedings, and for the moment Mabel was returned to her.

No longer in desperate financial straits, Annie was able to move to a bigger house in St John's Wood, shared with Mabel, the governess, and several women friends who rented rooms. No sooner had she moved than Bradlaugh, too, found his lodgings too cramped for himself and his two daughters, and he moved to within ten minutes' walk of her house. Scandal, of course, followed them; but in view of their characters, their passionately held moral beliefs and Annie's unhappy experience of marriage, it is unlikely that the two were lovers – or indeed that Annie Besant ever had a physical love-affair after she left her husband. At one point Frank Besant had her followed by detectives, but no evidence of the kind he wanted was ever found. Stubborn and proud as she was, she may have got a certain pleasure out of scandalizing society while knowing that her standards were in fact irreproachable.

Nevertheless, in many ways the companionship of Besant and Bradlaugh was like a happy marriage, giving her confidence and purpose and even making her laugh. 'He never spoke a harsh word,' she wrote, thinking, perhaps, of a contrast with Frank Besant:

Where we differed, he never tried to override my judgement, nor force on me his views; we discussed all points of difference as equal friends; he guarded me from all suffering as far as a friend might, and shared with me all the pain he could not turn aside; all the brightness of my stormy life came to me through him, from his tender thoughtfulness, his ever-ready sympathy, his generous love.

After his 'surgery' for free legal advice to the poor, he would bring his papers to Annie's house and they would work side-by-side through the day, exchanging a word now and then, breaking off for meals, working on until late evening in tacit comradeship. Sometimes they would take a day off and go exploring London or make excursions, ending up with tea and watercress in a little shop in Kew. Bradlaugh was a great fisherman and they spent days by the river, Annie taking instruction in the finer points of fishing. He softened the bitterness that had begun to stiffen her, warmed her and honoured her, and she was never to deny the debt she owed him.

In their views at this time they were in close agreement. On the questions of the day, Annie Besant was perpetually engaged in expounding the radical, subversive position. She was of course a champion of women and an advocate of women's suffrage, pointing out tartly that at the marriage ceremony the bridegroom promised to endow his bride with all his worldly goods while in fact appropriating all hers. She was anti-imperialist and criticized the government's aggressive policies in India, South Africa, Egypt. She was for Home Rule in Ireland. She was a republican, considering it merely a matter of time before royalty was abolished, and wanted to see the end of the House of Lords as well. Agricultural land she believed should be held by the state, not by the private landlord. She of course opposed capital punishment, and she urged humane treatment of the criminal.

Against war, against capital punishment, against flogging, demanding national education instead of big guns, public libraries instead of warships – no wonder I was denounced as an agitator, a firebrand, and that all orthodox society turned up at me its most respectable nose.

CHAPTER FOUR

In the next two years of Annie Besant's life, orthodox society did more than turn up its nose at her. Embodied in the country's legal system, it fought her openly and savagely. One battle was lost, and one battle won.

The first great fight was the battle of the 'Knowlton pamphlet'. Knowlton, a Freethinking Boston doctor, had written a booklet some forty years earlier with the elegant title of *The Fruits of Philosophy* – a title giving little clue to the fact that it was about birth control, both theoretical and practical. Knowlton had been prosecuted for writing it and had served three months in jail, but the booklet continued to be openly sold in both Britain and the United States. In 1876 it was being sold by Charles Watts, who published the *National Reformer* and Besant's and Bradlaugh's writings; in that year a Bristol bookseller of doubtful reputation interleaved it with illustrations of his own, which were declared indecent by the police.

Watts became scared of prosecution, and wanted to avoid being punished for publication of a book he had hardly seen. Besant and Bradlaugh, however, saw a new cause ahead to fight for, and persuaded him to stand by the book as a matter of principle. He allowed himself to be examined at a Bristol court, but soon after refused to go on selling the book. Bradlaugh himself did not much like the book anyway; the moving spirit in engineering the battle was Annie.

Watts and his wife put up such an objection to being martyred for Knowlton's views that Besant and Bradlaugh withdrew all the printing business of the National Secular Society from Watts and set up as printers themselves. Funds were opened to defend the case, but Freethinkers were divided about the book's worth, birth control not being part of the package they had bought when joining the Society. Meanwhile Watts and his wife brought out pamphlets blaming Bradlaugh and – in particular – Besant for stirring up the storm. Many a Freethinker was jealous of Annie Besant and her influence over their leader. Bradlaugh's daughters were jealous of her closeness to their father, and Hypatia was to write in later life that Annie's crusade for the Knowlton pamphlet pushed Bradlaugh into it willy-nilly and estranged him from many old friends.

Watts eventually did plead guilty at the Old Bailey and was let off with a small fine. Bradlaugh and Annie were not going to let the issue be evaded, and under their new imprint they reprinted Knowlton with a preface claiming 'the right to publish all opinions, so that the public, enabled to see all sides of the question, may have the material for forming a sound judgement'. It was ready early in 1877, price sixpence, and the two openly informed the police of its publication, sending along some free copies. On publication day their tiny office was jammed, and some five hundred sixpenny pamphlets were sold in the first twenty minutes.

What was this inflammatory publication about? It consisted of four chapters, the first an argument for population control based on Malthus's work – without such control, the population could be expected to double three times over within the next century, Knowlton argued. The second described the 'organs of generation' and the process of conception. The last two chapters were the most controversial. In the third, Knowlton finally reached the actual means of controlling conception: withdrawal; the 'baudruche' (a 'covering of very delicate skin' used by the male); a sponge attached to a narrow ribbon, to be used by the woman; post-coital syringing with a chemical solution. And in the last chapter he discussed the 'reproductive instinct', harmless, he argued, if indulged temperately (though 'solitary gratification' might lead to insanity). Far from wanting to encourage 'illegal connection', his argument was that chastity would be preserved if young people were enabled to marry early without fear.

Publication day ended, and no one had come to arrest Besant and Bradlaugh. The two lawbreakers let the police know that they were at home for arrest the next day; but it was not until April that the officers of the law appeared and the two were taken to the local police station to be searched, measured, and put on the criminal records. They were taken on to the Guildhall and put in separate cells. Hypatia, meanwhile, had been told that when they came to arrest her father she must immediately go home and fetch Russell *On Crime and Misdemeanours*:

I flew off to St John's Wood, collected the great books, and caught the next train to the City. It was a warm morning, I was hot with running, and anxious, for I rather think that I had some sort of notion that 'Russell' was a sort of golden key to unlock all legal difficulties. City men in the train, going to their ordinary business, looked at me rather curiously as I sat in the carriage closely hugging those three bulky volumes (which would slip about on one another, for I had not stayed to tie them together) on criminal procedure, of all things for a girl of nineteen to be carrying about with her on a sunny April morning.

But my sister and I felt very, very lonely and very cold at heart as we sat in the dreary Police Court at the Guildhall – I hardly know how we got there – listening to cases of drunkenness or assault, and waiting, with a shudder of horror and disgust at the thought, for our father and Mrs Besant to come and take their places at that dock which we had seen occupied by some of the lowest specimens of London low life.

But the preliminaries went off very civilly. Testimony was given, witnesses subpoenaed, bail accepted, and the case adjourned; there was a second equally low-key hearing some weeks later. Annie had absolutely insisted that she appear in the dock beside Bradlaugh and conduct her own defence, and it is hard to imagine that anything would have dissuaded her. Finally in June 1877 they appeared together at the court of Queen's Bench before the Lord Chief Justice and the trial proper began.

The charge was outlined by the Solicitor-General himself. The defendants had unlawfully and wickedly devised to corrupt the morals of the young, and other subjects of the Queen, and to incite them to obscene, unnatural and immoral practices by publishing an indecent, lewd, filthy, bawdy and obscene book. The implication constantly harped on by the prosecution was that the book would encourage young people to have sexual intercourse scot-free before marriage. With histrionic displays of distaste the Solicitor-General read out extracts to illustrate the appalling obscenity of the pamphlet. The prosecution drew to a close, and it was for Annie to open the defence.

She spoke to the court, fluently and confidently, for two

days – a testimony of some 40,000 words. Not just to defend herself was she standing there, she said; she was speaking on behalf of all the oppressed and inarticulate poor.

'My clients are scattered up and down through the length and breadth of the land; I find them amongst the poor, amongst whom I have been so much; I find my clients amongst the fathers, who see their wage ever reducing, and prices ever rising; I find my clients amongst the mothers worn out with over-frequent child-bearing, and with two or three little ones around too young to guard themselves, while they have no time to guard them . . . Gentlemen, do you know the fate of so many of these children? – the little ones half starved because there is food enough for two but not enough for twelve; half clothed because the mother, no matter what her skill and care, cannot clothe them with the money brought home by the breadwinner of the family; brought up in ignorance, and ignorance means pauperism and crime – gentlemen, your happier circumstances have raised you above this suffering.'

What corrupt intent could there be in their decision to publish, she asked? She had nothing to gain, and much to lose. 'I risk my name, I risk my liberty; and it is not without deep and earnest thought that I have entered this struggle.' She emphasized – and the jury's verdict was to show that she made her point – that to obtain a conviction it must be shown that there was a deliberate and malicious intent to corrupt public morals. She turned to the definition of obscenity; perhaps they might consider that neither Shakespeare nor the Bible could safely be sold to the general public. And the issue of free and open discussion was a crucial one; all their lives the jury would remember the verdict they had chosen to give at the Knowlton trial. A verdict of guilty would put an end to open discussion of the population question.

With masterly skill she expounded Malthus's views on

population expansion, checked only at present by the dreadful rate of infant mortality among the poor. 'I hold that it is more moral to prevent the birth of children than it is after they are born to murder them as you do today by want of food, and air, and clothing, and sustenance.'

On the second day of the trial Annie resumed her defence by producing a letter from Professor Alexander Bain, the psychologist, stating the trial to be 'one of the most critical in the history of our liberties'. She talked once more of the appalling conditions of which she – unlike, doubtless, most of her audience – had seen so much; of the fact that the lack of a population check led to the very obscenities that she was accused of fostering – illegitimacy, incest, criminality. Women of the working classes were broken by repeated pregnancies and lived in fear of each one. She quoted scores of letters from mothers of ten or twelve children who begged her to protect their daughters from going through the same experiences as they themselves had had. As to the upper classes, young bachelors' delayed marriages led to the equally dreadful social blot of prostitution.

Annie wound up her *tour de force* rousingly. Unless the jury believed that she had spoken nothing but a mass of falsehoods, that she was deliberately trying to corrupt the young under the guise of idealism, unless they believed that she deserved to be branded for life as false and vicious – 'I ask you, as an Englishwoman, for that justice which it is not impossible to expect at the hands of Englishmen – I ask you to give me a verdict of "Not Guilty" and send me home unstained.'

She won a round of applause, quickly suppressed. Sitting in the court through the trial was a young and unknown journalist, Bernard Shaw, who was later to play an important part in Annie Besant's life. Bradlaugh's teen-age daughters were conspicuously absent; their father had forbidden them to attend, as the subject-matter was not suitable for their ears.

Bradlaugh spoke after Annie, at rather less length, re-emphasizing some of her points and going more fully into legal technicalities 'I know the poor,' he concluded,

'I belong to them. I was born amongst them. Among them are the earliest associations of my life. Such little ability as I possess today has come to me in the hard struggle of life. I have had no University to polish my tongue; no Alma Mater to give me any eloquence by which to move you. I plead here simply for the class to which I belong, and for the right to tell them what may redeem their poverty and alleviate their misery.'

After the two principals had spoken, they called medical witnesses to substantiate the sufferings of working-class women under repeated pregnancies and to point out that the children of the poor died three times as fast as those of the rich. Annie and Bradlaugh concluded eloquently for the defence, and the Lord Chief Justice summed up. On one point, he said, everyone who had attended the trial should agree: 'A more ill-advised and more injudicious proceeding in the way of prosecution was probably never brought into a court of justice.' He proceeded with fine impartiality to outline the issues for the jury to consider. Both Annie and Bradlaugh felt it to have been a fair and favourable speech, and believed their case to be won.

But when the jurymen finally returned to the court after their deliberations their verdict was an odd compromise, much influenced by two extremely hostile members. 'We are unanimously of opinion that the book in question is calculated to deprave public morals,' said the foreman, 'but at the same time we entirely exonerate the defendants from any corrupt motives in publishing it.' The Lord Chief Justice was nonplussed; he could only direct the jury that what their verdict amounted to was 'Guilty'. The jury had agreed that if the verdict was not accepted as phrased, it would retire for further deliberation, but the foreman – one of the hostile two – seized the opportunity to let the 'Guilty' verdict pass. The rest of the jury remained stunned and passive – and the verdict stood.

The defendants were temporarily set free, agreeing to appear a week later for the judgement. At the weekend the Hall of Science was crowded, with people jamming the street outside. Besant and Bradlaugh were cheered; Annie announced that Bradlaugh intended to quash the verdict on the grounds of bad law. If all appeals failed, they would undergo the punishment assigned to them.

When they reappeared in court argument followed counter-argument. After a long day of struggle, the Lord Chief Justice delivered his verdict: they were to pay fines – and they were to go to prison for six months. 'I do not think we altogether realized what imprisonment could mean until the Judge pronounced the awful words,' wrote Hypatia Bradlaugh. 'The whole court seemed to fade away as I listened.' Besant and Bradlaugh had almost reached the door when the judge spoke again: if they would agree at least temporarily not to sell the book, they would be set free on their own recognizance of £100 each. They accepted the terms, and at the Court of Appeal the indictment was quashed on a technical point. It meant, at last, victory.

Annie meanwhile wrote her own birth-control pamphlet, in a style 'less coarse' than Knowlton's. The trial brought the subject out into the open and public discussion was unleashed. Both pamphlets sold over a hundred thousand copies and Annie's was translated into several languages. Ironically, she was to withdraw it herself in 1891. In accordance with Theosophical principles, her views had changed: 'By none other road than that of self-control and self-denial,' she then proclaimed, 'can men and women now set going the causes which will build for them brains and bodies of a higher type for their future return to earth-life.' It is perhaps a view that comes easier in middle age than in youth.

A terrible price remained to be paid for the victorious conclusion to the Knowlton battle. The year 1877, Annie Besant says in her autobiography, began with a struggle that ended in victory – but brought with it 'pain and anguish that I scarcely care to recall'. The notoriety of the trial enabled Frank Besant to make another attempt to take Mabel away from her mother, not content with having kept their son. This time he was to be successful.

Annie was nursing Mabel through scarlet fever when her husband's petition was delivered to her. It was claimed that his wife had propagated the principles of atheism through lectures and writings, that she had associated herself with an infidel lecturer and author named Charles Bradlaugh, and that she had published an indecent and obscene pamphlet. She was therefore not a fit person to be in charge of her daughter. Though the first and last of these accusations were the grounds on which she lost Mabel, the hint of scandal about her relationship to Bradlaugh no doubt played a covert part in the proceedings.

The case was heard by the Master of the Rolls, Sir George Jessel, a harsh and prejudiced man very unlike the Lord

Chief Justice who had presided over the Knowlton trial. From the start he expressed disgust at the idea of a woman's exposing herself by defending herself in a law court. The allegations were that Mabel would be 'outcast in this life and damned in the next' if she were allowed to stay in her mother's care. Witnesses testified to the education and the loving care that Mabel was receiving. Annie argued that her husband had been kept informed from the start about her views and activities, but Jessel was unshakably hostile. The verdict was that 'the child ought not to remain another day under the care of her mother'. Mabel was taken away. Annie appealed, and during the strain of waiting to hear the result fell ill with stress, grateful for 'the rest of pain and delirium instead of the agony of conscious loss'.

Legal sparring dragged on throughout the summer and autumn. Then Jessel, surprisingly, suggested that Annie file a claim for divorce. Annie claimed cruelty on Frank's part during their marriage; Frank categorically denied it. The legal conclusion was that by agreeing to the earlier separation she had lost her chance of divorce. It was too late. In a final hearing Jessel outlined the terms of her future relationship to her children: they might write to her; she could see them once a month; they could visit her twice a year; and once a year all three could spend a holiday together chaperoned by someone selected by their father.

But Mabel was terribly upset by her mother's rare visits; finally Annie, for their own sake, cut all ties with her children. 'It's a pity there isn't a God,' she had said when she left the courtroom that had taken them from her. 'It would do one so much good to hate Him.'

CHAPTER FIVE

The unforgivable taking away of her children would have broken the spirit of many women. At this point in her life Annie Besant might have succumbed to one of those mysterious Victorian 'low fevers' or undiagnosable ailments that so often confined nineteenth-century ladies to sofas and shawls. The loss of Mabel was an agony to her; well cared for in her absence, Mabel was always there to come home to after days of campaigning, to sleep in her bedroom beside her. 'She was the sweetness and joy of my life, my curly-headed darling, with her red-gold hair and glorious eyes, and passionate, wilful, loving nature.' There were to be no sofas or fevers, however. The titles of the chapters covering the next few years in her autobiography – 'At War All Round', 'Mr Bradlaugh's Struggle', 'Still Fighting' – speak for themselves. But it was perhaps around this time that work became less a joy than a drug, something that for the rest of her life she could not do without.

In the years 1878 and 1879, while she fought in the courts to regain custody of Mabel, she was putting together her writings on the French Revolution; translating a book from the French; keeping up her weekly journalism; producing pamphlets on atheism, republicanism, India and

Ireland; sitting on committees; and, of course, continuing to lecture. But it was not enough. 'I found that in my reading I developed a tendency to let my thoughts wander from the subject in hand, and that they would drift after my lost little one'; she decided, therefore, to 'occupy' herself by tackling a degree in science. And 'let me say to anyone in mental trouble,' she advised, 'that they might find an immense relief in taking up some intellectual recreation of this kind'. From her fruitless struggles in the courts for Mabel she 'found it the very greatest relief to turn to algebra, geometry and physics, and forget the harassing legal struggles in wrestling with formulae and problems'.

It helped her, too, to give her feelings against Christianity full rein now; 'the pamphlets written at this time against Christianity were marked with considerable bitterness, for it was Christianity that had robbed me of my child, and I struck mercilessly at it in return'. She was not alone in her bitterness at the blow that had been dealt her. The Free-thinkers were of course on her side, but some of the news-papers also took her part. 'The effect of their judgement is cruel,' said a Manchester paper, 'and it shows that the holding of unpopular opinions is, in the eye of the law, an offence which, despite all we had thought to the contrary, may be visited with the severest punishment a woman and a mother can be possibly called on to bear.'

It was not actually until 1878 that London University had approved a charter admitting women to its degrees – needless to say, after much opposition. Annie passed the preliminary tests with first-class honours, and then, to-gether with Hypatia and Alice Bradlaugh, plunged into a range of scientific courses. While she learned, she taught; by 1880 she had certificates qualifying her to lecture on chemistry, botany, mathematics, physiology and basic physics, and she held classes at the Hall of Science. She passed her first B.Sc. and the Preliminary Science examinations with honours. But, curiously, she continued to fail in practical chemistry, and this cost her her degree.

Prejudice was running so high against her and against the Bradlaugh girls that it is not impossible that the examiners deliberately failed her at this last hurdle. When she and Hypatia applied to attend the botany class at University College they were refused; a petition was got up and signed by eminent people and a Council meeting extraordinary was convened, but all attempts to change the ruling were voted down. When Annie – the only woman in Great Britain with first class honours in botany — asked permission to go into the Botanical Gardens in Regent's Park out of hours the curator refused it, on the grounds that his daughters sometimes walked there. A magnanimous botanist sent a ticket for Kew Gardens, however, with the stipulation that she avoid public visiting hours. Birkbeck College omitted her name from its list of successful examinees, and when she pointed out their mistake to them she was told that it had been deliberately left out in case contributors to their funds were deterred by seeing it. Mabel had to be led weeping out of church when she heard her mother referred to in a sermon as 'vile trash'. The martyrdom of which Annie had daydreamed as a girl was being carried out with a vengeance, and was perhaps not quite so straightforwardly satisfying as it had seemed in fantasy.

Meanwhile a new and not very benign influence had entered her life. Besant and Bradlaugh had been comrades, co-fighters, and (in the then current meaning of the word) lovers; Annie had referred to being 'engaged' to Mr Bradlaugh. Now the duo was to become a threesome, nicknamed 'the Trinity'. The newcomer was Dr Edward Aveling, lecturer in science.

Hypatia Bradlaugh, always a little feline in her comments on Annie, wrote of Annie's studies that 'it was Science which attracted her, as exemplified in the person of Dr Aveling' (Annie was always to be accused, not entirely without truth, of taking her latest set of beliefs from the latest strong personality she had encountered). We do not know, any more than with Bradlaugh, whether Annie and Aveling were lovers in the modern sense, but it is unlikely. Clearly, though, she was attracted and even fascinated by him for a time. 'As his friends closed their doors on him,' she wrote, 'I opened mine, and save for the time that he was with his pupils and night time, he made my house his home. All his work was carried on with me.'

Aveling was four years younger than Annie Besant and, like her, tied to a spouse he could not divorce. He was one of those characters who are attractive to women despite being cordially loathed by those not under his spell. Bernard Shaw, describing Aveling to his biographer, remarked that

as a borrower of money and a swindler and seducer of women his record was unimpeachable. On the same day he would borrow sixpence from the poorest man within his reach on the pretence of having forgotten his purse, and three hundred pounds from the richest to free himself from debts that he never paid. He had the art of coaching for science examinations, and girl students would scrape money together to pay him in advance his fee for twelve lessons. The more fortunate ones got nothing worse for their money than letters of apology for breaking the lesson engagements. The others were seduced and had their microscopes appropriated.

Strong words – but others reacted in the same way. The South African writer Olive Schreiner wrote later: 'I am beginning to have such a horror of Dr Aveling. To say I dislike him doesn't express it at all. I have a fear and a horror of him when I am near.'

Perhaps Annie was growing a little tired of Bradlaugh's high-mindedness. Perhaps she had hoped they could eventually marry, and was more shattered by the refusal of her divorce than she admitted. At any rate Bradlaugh now came gradually to fill the role of father or elder brother rather than that of fiancé. What he really felt about becoming part of a 'Trinity' we cannot be sure, but Hypatia wrote that her father's first disappointment in Mrs Besant was 'her intimacy with Dr Aveling'.

At any rate, from being Bradlaugh's protégée Annie was now in the position of having Aveling as the protégé of her own fame and influence. She encouraged him to lecture and teach at the Hall of Science, and she encouraged his writing. She was now editor of her own journal. At the beginning of 1883 the first issue of *Our Corner* came out, price sixpence, and containing fiction, essays, poetry and 'corners' of every kind – gardening corner, chess corner, puzzle corner, science corner. A particular claim to remembrance is that Shaw's two early novels appeared in it. A sort of courtship in print can be read between the lines of *Our Corner* and the *Reformer*. 'The most intense form of affection conceivable would be between a man and woman who both believed fully in the happier future of humanity and were both toiling to bring about that desired end,' wrote Aveling (purely hypothetically) in *Our Corner*. In the *Reformer* Besant was writing that the Hall of Science had acquired a lecturer of 'artistic charm' and 'brilliancy of brain'. Aveling's 'Holiday Musing' in *Our Corner* described Annie's favourite resort in Wales and continued:

Lo! from hills far asunder from those that had given it birth, another stream had been struggling to meet this ... It also has triumphed. For both the season of doubt and struggle is now over, and these twain ... flow into each other – as two noble lives – and move onwards to the sea, making a new gladness and beauty in the earth.

Two lives were indeed to flow into each other, but fortunately for Annie hers was not one of them. In the summer of 1884 Aveling swept off Eleanor Marx, daughter of Karl, to live in a 'free union'. Beatrice Webb has described Eleanor Marx in her journal:

Went in afternoon to British Museum and met Miss Marx in refreshment rooms ... '*We* think the Christian religion an *immoral illusion* and we wish to use *any* argument to persuade the people that it is false' ... Thought that Christ, if he had existed, was a weak-headed individual with a good deal of sweetness of character but quite lacking in heroism ... In person she is comely, dressed in a slovenly picturesque way with curly black hair flying about in all directions ... Lives alone, is much connected with Bradlaugh set, evidently peculiar views on love, etc., and I should think has somewhat 'natural' relations with men! Should fear that the chances were against her remaining long within the pale of 're-spectable' society.

Beatrice was right. It was indeed only a year later that Eleanor left 'respectable' society. She lived with Aveling for fourteen years, and committed suicide when he made a legal marriage to a girl of twenty-two.

*

53

Meanwhile Bradlaugh had other things to think of than his changing relationship with Annie. The years 1880 to 1886 were the years of his heartbreaking, farcical struggle with the House of Commons. He was elected to the Commons as member for Northampton in 1880, the first declared atheist to be sent to Parliament. 'A very madness of tumultuous delight' was how Annie described the scenes in Nottingham; 'the mass of men and women, one sea of heads from hotel to station, every window crowded, his colours waving everywhere, men fighting to get near him, to touch him, women sobbing, the cries, "Our Charlie, our Charlie; we've got you and we'll keep you".'

But it was the beginning, not the end, of a long fight. As an atheist Bradlaugh wished to 'affirm' to Parliament rather than be sworn in on the Bible, and had the legal right to do so. He presented his case to the House, and it was rejected. Twice he was refused permission to take his seat, then taken into custody, then set free. The issue became a *cause célèbre* of civil rights, as the Knowlton pamphlet had.

In the summer of 1881 he determined simply to take his seat. The House of Commons was virtually in a state of siege, with reserves of police packed inside and the angry Bradlaughites outside. When the crowd tried to storm the staircase Annie – later regretting it – turned them peaceably back. Bradlaugh eventually appeared, pale and dishevelled; he had been dragged out forcibly by a group of policemen. He was in many ways a conventional man; he had believed devoutly in the rule of law and in parliamentary government, and Annie Besant in her autobiography claims that the treachery of the House of Commons broke his spirit. 'He never dreamed that, going alone amongst his foes, ready to submit to expulsion, to imprisonment ... that they would use brutal and cowardly violence, and shame every Parliamentary tradition.'

The fight was to continue for several more years. When Bradlaugh did take his seat unopposed he was tired, in debt and beginning to age. But a Bill allowing members the right to affirm ensured that no member of Parliament ever again had to go through what he had experienced.

Through these years of sweat and struggle in the early 1880s a faint note, like the disembodied bells that the medium Helena Blavatsky set chiming, was coming from overseas. The *National Reformer* carried advertisements for the *Theosophist*; news came that members of the National Secular Society in India were joining the Theosophical Society; Madame Blavatsky angled in the *Theosophist*'s columns for comradeship between English Freethinkers and her organization – for were they not both opponents of Christianity? Bradlaugh had even met and liked Blavatsky's co-leader, Colonel Olcott, when he was in the United States. But both Bradlaugh and Besant disowned Theosophy in print, and privately advised members of the National Secular Society not to join. 'There is a radical difference between the mysticism of Theosophy and the scientific materialism of Secularism. The exclusive devotion to this world implied in the profession of Secularism leaves no room for other-worldism.'

The jocular Freethought attitude to Theosophy at this time was summed up in Bradlaugh's reference to a scandalous piece of cheating by substitution in which the Theosophical Society had been caught out. 'We see that Theosophy includes miracle working, even to the extent of restoring a broken china plate to its perfect state without cement or patching. A Theosophical housemaid ought to be a desideratum in a household where there are many breakages.'

CHAPTER SIX

Besant and Bradlaugh, the once inseparable comrades, were to draw yet further apart; for Annie Besant now made a significant shift in political allegiance. The combination of the two had been so extraordinary, wrote Bernard Shaw, that 'its dissolution was felt as a calamity, as if some one had blown up Niagara or an earthquake had swallowed a cathedral'. Annie deserted Bradlaugh's radicalism for socialism, first as embodied in the moderate form of the Fabian Society.

Why Bradlaugh, with his subversive views on everything from religion to foreign policy, was not a socialist himself needs some explaining today. He was, said Annie in her autobiography, 'nurtured on self-reliant individualism', and did not see that the socialism of the 1880s was a new phenomenon. He was against any kind of class warfare, believing that the struggle for reform should be an inter-class movement; and he remembered the blood shed for the Paris Commune. Socialism, to the Bradlaughite radical, meant class war and state control as opposed to individual freedom.

Annie Besant was younger and more fluid – sometimes alarmingly fluid – in her ideas. It seems inevitable that she should have eventually followed her political and social beliefs through to their logical conclusion; indeed, she declared that it was only the hostility between the Bradlaugh faction and the socialist groups that held her back for so long. In the spring of 1884 a debate – 'Will Socialism Benefit the English People?' – was staged between Bradlaugh and the socialist H. M. Hyndman and, seemingly, the experienced Bradlaugh carried the day. It left Annie thinking, however. Already, a year before, she had carried an article defending socialism in *Our Corner*. Throughout 1884 she 'listened, read and thought much, but said little'. 'Slowly,' she says, 'I found that the case for Socialism was intellectually complete and ethically beautiful.'

Soon after she was writing in full Besantine vigour:

Christian charity? We know its work. It gives a hundredweight of coal and five pounds of beef once a year to a family whose head could earn a hundred such doles if Christian justice allowed him fair wage for the work he performs. It plunders the workers of the wealth they make, and then flings back at them a thousandth part of their own product as 'charity'.

The socialist paper *Justice* had already twitted her: 'Mrs Besant is finding it necessary to turn Socialist; but does not like anyone to tell her so.' She hesitated, still, to make her change of allegiance public, and so bring herself 'into collision with the dearest of my friends' and 'strain the strong and tender tie so long existing'. But

the cry of starving children was ever in my ears; the sobs of women poisoned in lead works, exhausted in nail works, driven to prostitution by starvation, made old and haggard by ceaseless work. I saw their misery was the result of an evil system, was inseparable from private ownership of the instruments of wealth production;

that while the worker was himself but an instrument, selling his labour under the law of supply and demand, he must remain helpless in the grip of the employing classes.

It was in the summer of 1885 that the moment for disclosure came, dramatic as always. Bernard Shaw was addressing the Dialectical Society on socialism, and was perturbed to see Annie Besant in the audience. He assumed that she had come to crush him, and prepared to meet his fate. When the time came for the opposition to state its case, however, Annie remained silent and someone else led the field. When he had finished, she stood up and supported Shaw. Such was her public announcement of her new allegiance. After the meeting she asked Shaw to nominate her for membership of the Fabians.

It is a moot question how far Shaw influenced her political shift, as Aveling had influenced her dedication to science. She herself replied indignantly to a critic accusing her of feminine inconstancy that she did not even know her socialist colleagues until she had made her decision; 'The moment a man uses a woman's sex to discredit her arguments, the thoughtful reader knows that he is unable to answer the arguments themselves. But really these silly sneers at woman's ability have lost their force, and are best met with a laugh at the stupendous "male self-conceit" of the writer.'

She did, however, at least meet Shaw as early as 1884, when in a debate he introduced himself as a 'loafer'. 'I was fairly astounded at the audacious confession that he led so shameful a life,' thundered Annie in her newspaper column. 'The only fair answer would be: "Go and work, before you set yourself up to teach workers".' When she learned that, poor as he was, he worked long unpaid hours for the causes he believed in, she admitted that she felt cross and foolish. She was never to understand his sense of humour.

At the time of this first meeting Shaw was twenty-nine, awkward, unknown and impoverished, and Annie at thirty-eight was at the height of her fame. It was a year or two later, when she had joined his cause, that the friendship really ripened into a platonic, teasing flirtation, serious on her side but not on his. What Annie did not know was that Shaw was highly skilled at platonic, teasing friendships; he kept several simmering during the period of their acquaintance, as well as one non-platonic one with a widow fifteen years older than himself. He disliked himself for this compulsive game, even though he managed, curiously, always to be the pursued rather than the pursuer; reading over Annie's letters, he recorded in his diary that he was 'rather disgusted with the trifling of the last two years with women'. Nevertheless he liked her and understood her as few of the people who had surrounded her had done.

The key to her character, he said, was pride; she had to be the giver and not the taker, the leader rather than the led. She was extremely generous to Shaw and he knew it, as she paid him for his contributions to *Our Corner* out of her own pocket when she realized how poor he was. He loved her for it, but shrewdly saw even beneficence as a kind of pride. Just so had Pusey said to her when she went to ask for his religious guidance, 'You are full of spiritual pride' – or, more charitably, of independence and courage. She was never pompous or power-obsessed, yet there was a bitter kernel in her life somewhere – perhaps just in being younger sister to the never-mentioned brother – which drove her to be always first.

Intensely serious she certainly was. Shaw wrote that he succeeded in making her laugh at him, but not at herself; she did have 'a healthy sense of fun', but 'comedy was not her clue to life'. 'The apparently heartless levity with which I spoke and acted in matters which were deeply serious . . . must have made it very hard for her to work with me at times,' Shaw was to write with unconvincing modesty. Her temperament was a natural target for the Shavian arrow. Raina in *Arms and the Man*, he told a biographer, was based on Annie; Raina, high-minded but as hypocritical as only a Shavian heroine can be, whose bluff is called by the down-to-earth Bluntschli:

RAINA: . . . You know, I've always gone on like that.
BLUNTSCHLI: You mean the – ?
RAINA: I mean the noble attitude and the thrilling voice. [*They laugh together.*] I did it when I was a tiny child to my nurse. She believed in it. I do it before my parents. They believe in it. I do it before Sergius. He believes in it.

Between 1885 and 1887 Annie was certainly serious about Shaw. They played piano duets together and she wrote poems as well as letters to him. Unable as she was to marry legally, at one point in their friendship she drew up a contract for a 'free union' like that of Eleanor Marx and Aveling. His reaction, according to Shaw himself, was: 'Good God! This is worse than all the vows of the churches on earth. I had rather be legally married to you ten times over.' He was a slippery fish, after the puritanical but straightforward Bradlaugh and the stage-villain Aveling, and Annie was quite out of her depth. There were tears, and letters were demanded and sent back. In his diary Shaw congratulated himself that though the friendship, through his own fault, had 'threatened to become a vulgar intrigue . . . I roused myself in time and avoided this'. At the time, no doubt, it was little consolation to Annie that his admiration for her was genuine and durable.

Among the Fabians she was at first a little out of place. They were gradualists, not heroes, concerned with drains and taxes rather than metaphysics. The great atheist cause dwindled in importance; mostly, they were uninterested in absolutes. And the intellectual standard among these donnish people was perhaps higher than it had been among the Freethinkers. Clear thought, rather than oratorical passion, was what was demanded. Clear thought and a sense of the comic; 'we laughed at Socialism and laughed at ourselves a good deal,' said Shaw. But Annie soon found her particular niche. She became, Shaw continues,

a sort of expeditionary force, always to the front when there was trouble and danger, carrying away audiences for us when the dissensions in the movement brought our policy into conflict with that of the other societies, founding branches for us throughout the country, dashing into the great strikes and free speech agitations . . . and generally leaving the routine to us and taking the fighting on herself.

The day came when Annie's fighting spirit was to be well and truly tested. The year 1886 saw the beginning of a depression – for the worker, not the investor; dividends were high, but the number of unemployed was steadily growing. A 'strong' Conservative government clamped down hard on signs of unrest; socialist outdoor speakers were attacked by the police, and a fund for bail and legal advice had to be set up. Throughout 1887 conditions worsened. 'This one thing is clear,' wrote Annie, 'Society must deal with the unemployed, or the unemployed will deal with Society.'

Autumn brought a crisis. Desperate at the prospect of another hungry winter, the London unemployed began to hold street marches and meetings in Trafalgar Square. Repeatedly the police closed in on demonstrators and dispersed them. A march and meeting was planned for Sunday, 13 November 1887. Suddenly, on the Saturday night, the Commissioner of Police issued an order forbidding any organized procession to approach the Square. Annie Besant was among those who urged that they should use their legal right to free speech and go ahead with the demonstration.

On a grey Sunday, as marchers approached the Square from all directions, some 1,600 police were waiting for them. A number of the processions were broken up before they ever reached it; there was fighting in Holborn and the Strand, with injuries on both sides. By afternoon, though, a solid mass of marchers had reached Trafalgar Square, and the police, supplemented by troops, went into action. 'Then ensued a scene to be remembered; the horse police charged in squadrons at a hand-gallop, rolling men and women over like ninepins, while the foot police struck recklessly with their truncheons, cutting a road through the crowd that closed immediately behind them.' A hundred and thirty people injured by hoof or baton had to be admitted to hospital, and two died from their injuries.

Annie could do little as 'Bloody Sunday' unfolded, though she tried unsuccessfully to break a charge of mounted police by obstruction. Once it was over, however, she went into action, organizing defence and bail for the hundred or so who had been imprisoned. With W. T. Stead, editor of the *Pall Mall Gazette*, she set up a Law and Liberty League across the country to resist government and police intimidation. The following Sunday, a crowd gathered spontaneously in the Square and again was charged by the police. One man, Alfred Linnell, was so badly trampled that he died some days later. Annie and others arranged a funeral that would not be forgotten, the cortège led by herself, Stead and other socialist leaders, and the coffin inscribed: 'Died from injuries inflicted by the police'.

Annie and Stead were now to work closely together. Stead, at thirty-nine two years younger than Annie, was what we would now call an investigative journalist. His *Pall Mall Gazette* had carried exposures, scandals and attacks that had made him famous. He was on the side of the underdog; and, though a Christian, he tremendously admired Annie Besant. Together they founded *The Link*, a halfpenny weekly which carried on its front page a quotation from Victor Hugo: 'I will speak for the dumb. I will speak of the small to the great and of the feeble to the strong ... I will speak for all the despairing silent ones.' *The Link* attacked sweated labour, extortionate landlords, unhealthy workshops, child labour, and prostitution.

In the summer of 1888 the paper printed a sensational article by Annie entitled 'White Slavery in London', exposing the working conditions of the women in Bryant and May's match factory. 'It is time someone came and helped us,' said one of the girls to her, and she accepted the challenge. The firm was paying a dividend of 38 per cent, but women employees were getting an average of seven shillings for a sixty-hour week spent in unhealthy conditions. Annie held a protest meeting, and the match-girls, 1,400 strong, voted to come out on strike.

Private contributions supported the girls while they were

out. A boycott of Bryant and May's matches was urged; a poem called 'The Match-maker's Complaint' was printed; public meetings were held, articles written, and questions were asked in Parliament by Bradlaugh. 'The girls behaved splendidly, stuck together, kept brave and bright all through,' wrote Annie. The company meanwhile fought hard, but the exposé had aroused the sympathy of public and press. It had to retreat; the women were taken back, at an only slightly higher wage but with a guarantee of improved working conditions. The factory became a model workplace, with a strong and independent union of which Annie was Honorary Secretary. The financial gains of the strike may have been slight, but it was a great step forward for trade unionism.

Annie now interested herself in the working conditions of box-makers, fur-pullers and dockers, among others:

. . . a finisher of boots paid 2s. 6d. per dozen pairs and 'find your own polish and thread'; women working for 10½ hours per day, making shirts – 'fancy best' – at from 10d. to 3s. per dozen, finding their own cotton and needles, paying for gas, towel, and tea (compulsory), earning from 4s. to 10s. per week for the most part; a mantle finisher 2s. 2d. per week, out of which 6d. for materials . . .

By this time she had probably seen more of the poor's way of life than any other woman of her class in the country. 'Oh, those trudges through the lanes and alleys round Bethnal Green Junction late at night, when our day's work was over,' she wrote; 'children lying about on shavings, rags, anything; famine looking out of baby faces, out of women's eyes, out of the tremulous hands of men.'

There was yet another iron in the fire. Now a member of the more left-wing Social Democratic group, she campaigned through the summer and autumn of 1888 for election to the London School Board in Tower Hamlets (she had wanted to run for the new London County Council, but women were excluded). Her programme was free secular education and free meals – 'if we insist on these children being educated, is it not necessary that they shall be fed?' Up and down the East End she addressed meetings, supported by Freethought and socialist comrades. Churchmen held meetings to speak against her; but when the votes were in she stood at the top of the poll with a majority of nearly 3,000.

It has been said that her work on the London School Board was in fact the most solid achievement of her career. She laid the foundations of the school medical services and by the end of 1889 had conjured up, by her own estimate, 36,000 school dinners. In that year too she significantly forwarded the principles of trade unionism when the Board had a contract to assign. She argued that trade-union wages should be a condition of the contract, and won her point. The Board was thus the first public body to insist that all contractors pay their workers a fair wage.

But beyond all this public activity Annie Besant was thinking of other things than union rates and free dinners. Some of them, listed by her later, were hypnosis, dreams, the body–mind relation, memory, thought transference, spiritualism and clairvoyance. She felt that the question, 'Where to gain the inspiration, the motive, which should lead to the realization of the Brotherhood of Man?' still lacked an answer. And she was not happy. Her friend Stead, a religious man who understood her deeply religious nature, said that throughout this time she was sick at heart and in love with death.

CHAPTER SEVEN

Fittingly, Annie was to make the chapter on her conversion
to Theosophy – 'From Storm to Peace' – the last one in her
autobiography. In 1889 she left behind her a whole life,
and started a new one.* The story of her conversion must be
told in her own words; the 'noble attitude and the thrilling
voice' that Raina admits to were never more in evidence.

She had been dissatisfied for years, she wrote. 'Heart grew
sick, and eyes dim, and ever louder sounded the question,
"Where is the cure for sorrow, what the way of rescue for
the world?".' But, at last,

sitting alone in deep thought as I had become accustomed to do
after the sun had set, filled with an intense but nearly hopeless
longing to solve the riddle of life and mind, I heard a Voice that
was later to become to me the holiest sound on earth, bidding me
take courage for the light was near.

It was; Stead was to pass her the two volumes of Madame
Blavatsky's *The Secret Doctrine* for review. Other reviewers
had quailed, but Annie was considered 'quite mad enough

---

* It will be clear that Theosophists, of whom there are still a large
number in many countries, maintain a different version of events related in
this and subsequent chapters.

on these subjects' to cope – proof that her growing interest in the occult was known to friends. She set about the task, not without humour – 'I am immersed in Madame Blavatsky! If I perish in the attempt to review her, you must write on my tomb, "She has gone to investigate the Secret Doctrine at first hand".'

In a sense the old Annie did perish on the way, giving birth to a new one. For in spite of the length and obscurity of the books, she was 'dazzled, blinded by the light in which disjointed facts were seen as parts of a mighty whole, and all my puzzles, riddles, problems, seemed to disappear ... The light had been seen, and in that flash of illumination I knew that the weary search was over and the very Truth was found.' She proceeded to get an introduction to Madame Blavatsky from Stead, and with her friend Herbert Burrows went to 17 Lansdowne Road:

'My dear Mrs Besant, I have so long wished to see you', and I was standing with my hand in her firm grip, and looking for the first time in this life straight into the eyes of 'H.P.B.' I was conscious of a sudden leaping forth of my heart – was it recognition? – and then, I am ashamed to say, a fierce rebellion, a fierce withdrawal, as of some wild animal when it feels a mastering hand ... She talked of travels, of various countries, easy brilliant talk, her eyes veiled, her exquisitely moulded fingers rolling cigarettes incessantly ... We rose to go, and for a moment the veil lifted, and two brilliant, piercing eyes met mine, and with a yearning throb in the voice: 'Oh, my dear Mrs Besant, if you would only come among us!' I felt a well-nigh uncontrollable desire to bend down and kiss her, under the compulsion of that yearning voice, those compelling eyes, but with a flash of the old unbending pride and an inward jeer at my own folly, I said a commonplace polite goodbye ...

She saw the obstacles to the step she was going to take –

'Was I to plunge into a new vortex of strife, and make myself a mark for ridicule – worse than hatred – and fight again the weary fight for an unpopular truth?' Indeed, yes. Though Blavatsky had given Annie a damaging report on her miracles published by the Society for Psychical Research, Annie threw it aside with 'the righteous scorn of an honest nature that knew its own kin when it met them' and filled In her application to join the Theosophical Society. At Lansdowne Road she found Madame alone:

I went over to her, bent down and kissed her, but said no word. 'You have joined the Society?' 'Yes.' 'You have read the report?' 'Yes.' 'Well?' I knelt down before her and clasped her hands in mine, looking straight into her eyes. 'My answer is, will you accept me as your pupil, and give me the honour of proclaiming you my teacher in the face of the world?' Her stern, set face softened, the unwonted gleam of tears sprang to her eyes; then, with a dignity more than regal, she placed her hand upon my head. 'You are a noble woman. May Master bless you.'

Since then, Annie wrote four years later, her faith had never wavered. Master indeed blessed her. She had kept her appointment with truth:

That one loyalty to Truth I must keep stainless, whatever friendships fail me or human ties be broken. She may lead me into the wilderness, yet I must follow her; she may strip me of all love, yet I must pursue her; though she slay me, yet will I trust in her; and I ask no other epitaph on my tomb but
            'SHE TRIED TO FOLLOW TRUTH'.

What was the Theosophical truth that she now made her own? To understand it one must know something about its originator.

Helena Petrovna von Hahn was born into an aristocratic

Russian family in 1831, sixteen years before the birth of Annie Besant. Her mother was a novelist, who passed on her gift for romancing to her daughter. Helena was an unloved and difficult child who comforted herself with belief in her magical powers. At seventeen, in a fit of bravado or despair, she married the middle-aged Nikifor Blavatsky and after three months ran away from him.

Her life between that time and the founding of Theosophy exists in contradictory versions. According to her own, she went to Egypt to study with a Coptic magician, travelled in the States, Peru and Mexico in search of further occult knowledge, and met a Master from the Himalayas who told her she had been chosen for a mission to humanity. In Italy she fought under Garibaldi in male dress; in Burma, Siam and China she underwent further esoteric training; and in Tibet she took instruction from the hierarchy of Masters in a remote monastery.

We have associated with fakirs, the holy men of India and seen them in intercourse with the *Pitris*. We have watched the proceedings and *modus operandi* of the howling and dancing dervishes; held friendly communications with the marabouts of European and Asiatic Turkey; and the serpent-charmers of Damascus and Benares have but few secrets that we have not had the fortune to study.

The alternative version suggests that she lived and travelled with a singer, Agardi Metrovitch, and that she had a child either by Metrovitch or by a Count Meyendorff. He died at five years old and, like Annie Besant, Helena did not forgive the Christian God. In 1871 she and Metrovitch were in a shipwreck from which there were few survivors; Metrovitch died in it, and Helena landed penniless in

Cairo, where she set up a spiritualist group. Two years later, aged forty-one, she sailed for New York (by order, of course, of the Masters). From then on, fact and fantasy are easier to distinguish.

While Annie Besant was losing her Christian faith and leaving her husband, H.P.B., as she now liked to call herself, was trying to establish herself in New York. North America was at that time in the grip of a spiritualistic fever, and it was the obvious place for an occultist to settle in. But she was running short of money and contacts. One day she read an article – 'Astounding Wonders that Stagger Belief' – by Colonel Henry Olcott, ex-soldier, ex-lawyer, who was writing up spiritualism for the newspapers. She set out to meet him, and a partnership was born.

Olcott was worldly but restless for miracles, married but separated from his family. Helena Petrovna's abilities bowled him over, though by the time they set up home together he was under no illusions about her volatile Russian temper. It was not a sexual partnership; Olcott had mistresses, and H.P.B. had briefly 'married' an Armenian ten years her junior. By 1876 she and Olcott – Mulligan and Maloney, as they playfully called each other – were sharing an apartment on 47th Street. Helena was a lonely woman, and there was a genuine affection between the two, tinged with awe and resentment on his side and with contempt on hers. With Olcott as 'straight man', her psychic gifts – undoubtedly supplemented by practical conjuring – blossomed as never before and she produced 'phenomenon' after 'phenomenon' to dazzle him.

Still – money, as well as the mission that she really half believed in, remained the problem. 'Here, you see, is my trouble, tomorrow there will be nothing to eat,' she wrote to her friend Alexander Aksakoff. 'Something quite out of the way must be invented.'

It was invented almost by chance. H.P.B. and Olcott often held open house for discussions, and after a talk on Egyptian magic and elemental spirits Olcott suggested forming a Society for their studies. Various names – Hermetic, Rosi-crucian, Egyptological – were suggested before Theosophical was adopted. H.P.B. was not very interested, and Olcott was voted president. After a few months, membership had dropped almost to nil. Meanwhile H.P.B. was writing her first book, *Isis Unveiled*, on the dictation, she said, of her Masters:

> *Somebody* comes and envelops me as a misty cloud and all at once pushes me out of myself, and then I am not 'I' any more – Helena Petrovna Blavatsky – but someone else. Someone strong and powerful, born in a totally different region of the world . . .

The publication of *Isis Unveiled* brought its author letters from readers in various countries, and the idea grew that the defunct Society might be revived in India, home of much oriental lore incorporated into the book. H.P.B. hoped to amalgamate with an Indian society, the Arya Samaj, but on her arrival in India with Olcott, their guru rejected her as an ignoramus. Nevertheless, when she and Olcott started their journal the *Theosophist*, disciples both Indian and English began to be attracted. One of them was the influential editor A. P. Sinnett, whose books Annie Besant had read before she took on *The Secret Doctrine*. In the atmosphere of admira-tion, H.P.B.'s mediumistic phenomena – raps, chimes, the production of objects out of thin air – revived wonderfully and caused a sensation.

By this time she was firmly and disastrously committed to

the magical 'precipitation' of letters from her Masters, first
called the Brethren of Luxor but now located in Tibet and
named Master Koot Hoomi and Master Morya. Letters
appeared on desks and fell from ceilings, and to deal with
these and other miracles she needed help. Her accomplice
was an old friend from Cairo days, Emma Coulomb; as the
Society prospered and acquired headquarters, H.P.B. was
writing her incriminating letters:

> In the name of heaven, do not think I have forgotten you. I have
> not even time to breathe – that is all!! We are in the *greatest crisis*
> and *I must not* LOSE MY HEAD.
> . . . It is *absolutely necessary* that something should happen in
> Bombay while I am here. The King and Dam. must see one of the
> Brothers and receive a visit from him, and, if possible, the first
> must receive a letter which I shall send . . . The letter must fall on
> his head . . . We must strike while the iron is hot.

She was wise, later, to pre-empt criticism and give Annie
the Society for Psychical Research's report straight away. It
was compiled by Richard Hodgson, who went out to investigate the by now famous Madame in 1884. He inter-
viewed Theosophists, examined handwriting and receipts,
and collected evidence from the Coulombs. His conclusions
were unequivocal:

> We regard her neither as the mouthpiece of hidden seers, nor as
> a mere vulgar adventuress; we think that she has achieved a title
> to permanent remembrance as one of the most accomplished,
> ingenious, and interesting impostors in history.

A number of people seceded from the Society; but in the
end the triumphant march of Theosophy was not halted. By
the time Annie joined, *The Secret Doctrine* had come out,

another magazine was launched, and the London branch was flourishing.

Theosophy was extraordinarily successful because it filled a gap in the late nineteenth-century world that is now very apparent. Christianity was ostensibly still strong in the land, but its foundations had been shaken by Darwinism, and the more intelligent knew it. At the same time, it was an age when spiritualistic phenomena were flourishing and catching the attention of serious investigators. When the Society for Psychical Research was founded in 1882, it was headed not by nonentities but by Cambridge philosophers. Freud had not yet arrived, but there was a feeling that a new psychology contained many mysteries; William James's *Principles of Psychology*, published in 1890, devoted full chapters to hypnotism, the stream of thought and the consciousness of self. And the scraps of Buddhist and Hindu thought that were incorporated into Theosophy were exciting at a time when knowledge of comparative religions was confined to a handful of scholars. Along with these, a revival of occult traditions going back to neo-Platonism, Gnosticism, alchemy and Rosicrucianism was under way.

A new and exotic 'religion' was needed, and Theosophy had something for everybody. It managed to co-exist with the 'higher thought' generally – Fabianism, the Ethical Church, spiritualism and Theosophy rubbed shoulders, and Annie Besant was not the only one to dabble in them severally. Edith Lees, Havelock Ellis's wife, left in her novel *Attainment* a semi-fictional account of a co-operative she ran in the early 1900s. Characters include a poet, an anarchist, a botanist, and a Theosophist who is a 'developed soul'. Vegetarian food is served, a book on ethics lies open on a table; on the walls are pictures of Madame Blavatsky,

Queen Victoria, Goethe and Walt Whitman. 'We have tried to assimilate all the newer ideas of the day,' says one of the members.

Of course, part of Theosophy's success lay in the fact that it started from really *big* lies. Disbelievers had to maintain that the travelled and cultured Madame Blavatsky was cheating and forging on a large scale. It now seems certain that she was; but it is not all there was to her. Compared with the complexity of Helena Petrovna, Annie seems a schoolgirl in her simplicity. In H.P.B. there was genuine psychic ability and an untrammelled imagination, down-to-earth vulgarity and prudishness, vivacity and Russian melancholy. If she set a troublesome hoax going with her story of Masters and their secret missives, it was because she had believed, from her lonely childhood on, that she was under special protection; there were Masters somewhere who *did* care for her, even if for the moment she had to forge their letters. Hodgson had been so baffled by the pointlessness of her frauds that he thought she must be a Russian spy. In fact the big lies were told compulsively and with passionate emotion behind them, and it made them irresistible. Able, like so many nineteenth-century characters, to dissociate parts of herself, Helena believed the lies herself much of the time; at other times she felt isolated among dupes whom she despised. But she knew she had gifts as a medium, she knew she had learnt much occult lore on her travels, and the rest was the blissful exercise of imagination.

For *The Secret Doctrine* – subtitled 'The Synthesis of Science, Religion, Philosophy' – H.P.B. conjured up the Book of Dzyan, the oldest manuscript in the world, 'a collection of palm leaves made impermeable in water, fire, and air by some specific and unknown process', and written in Senzar, the secret language of initiates. The book contained an allegorical account of the genesis of all the universes:

Kosmos in Eternity, before the reawakening of still slumbering Energy, the Emanation of the World in later systems . . . It is the Point in the Mundane Egg, the Germ within it which will become the Universe, the All, the boundless, periodical Kosmos – a Germ which is latent and active, periodically and by turns.

And so on, through the PRESENCE, the Universal Soul, mantavaric manifestations and the Divine Thought.

Universes arise and decline through the outbreathings of this primordial spirit. They contain beings at every stage of evolution, from base spirits through men to evolved Masters. Worlds are created by the seven Dhyan-Chohans, who use universal electricity (Fohat). There have been four races on this earth before the present one: the First Root Race, the Hyperboreans, the Lemurians, and the Atlanteans. The present race, the Aryans, will die out and be replaced by two further races . . . And more, much more; hierarchies of seven (seven sub-races, root races, rounds, chains), seven elements in man, seven planes in the solar system; hierarchies of beings running the system – the Great White Brotherhood, the Lords of Karma.

Where did Blavatsky get it all from? Partly from what other science-fiction writers have used – imagination. Partly from books available on Hinduism and tantric Buddhism, partly from the Tradition, the underground esotericism drawn upon for many centuries and dating back to oriental mystery-religions. Blavatsky's claim was that all these sources came from the same fountainhead and could be combined together. 'The aim of this work,' she declared of *The Secret Doctrine*, was to show that Nature is not 'a fortuitious concurrence of atoms', and to assign to man his rightful place in the scheme of the Universe; to rescue from degradation the archaic truths which are the basis of all religions; to uncover, to some extent, the fundamental unity from which they all spring; finally, to show that the Occult side of Nature has never been approached by the Science of modern civilization.

In practice, Theosophists concerned themselves less with Dhyan-Chohans and Fohat than with the ideas of karma and rebirth, of a universal religion, of the 'astral' dimension, and, of course, with the Masters.

The idea of adepts, initiates, Boddhisatvas and avatars is an old one. If the universe is full of evolving beings from the lowest to the highest, there must be great souls who are on their way to a higher form. If true knowledge is a secret doctrine, there must be the few who pass on the lore. Underground knowledge has always had its fraternities and cults. In the 1840s the novelist Bulwer-Lytton drew on the idea for his *Zanoni*, in which only two members remain on earth of a brotherhood possessing the secret of eternal life. Later, the fashionable guru Gurdjieff drew on it – possibly via Theosophy – in describing a journey to the remote mountain monastery of the Brothers who instructed him. Rosicrucianism had its brotherhood of wise men.

When all the ludicrous terminology is cleared away, one can see what it was that satisfied Annie Besant in Theosophy. It allowed for her inherent religiosity by declaring that all creeds are only perversions of an original world Wisdom. It dealt with her dissatisfaction with materialism by predicating a universally spiritual nature to everything. It answered her questions about spiritualist and hypnotic phenomena by explaining that 'magic' is not outside nature but has always been part of the adept's skills. It supported her deep belief in the evolution and perfectability of man, through its fantasticated cosmology. And it dealt with her first and last grudge against God – the problem of pain, the cruelty of things – through the doctrine of karma and re-birth. Suffering was logical, not random, and only part of a long cycle of evolving lifetimes. '*You think people can hurt you. Then you do not believe in the law of Karma.* It is your own hand that strikes you, and no one else's. No one can injure you or wrong you, no one can commit any injustice against you.'

These were the reasons of the head for Annie, and there were undoubtedly reasons of the heart as well. She was perhaps simply bored with trade unionism and school administration, with her socialist colleagues and with her growing respectability. She needed to return to *credo quia impossibile*. Then, there was something of a (quite innocent) love-affair about her surrender to H.P.B. Men – her husband, Bradlaugh, Aveling, Shaw – had all let her down in some way, and she turned to Helena Petrovna as to a mother. She was too honest herself to believe that there were great streaks of fraud in Theosophy, and she was very literal; even before she took the great step, she had been puzzling, in a letter to a friend with whom she was conducting psychic experiments, about the Masters' treatment of Madame Blavatsky. (Yeats, it should be noticed, also dismissed the idea of the Masters being a fraud; if not living men, they must be, he wrote, 'dramatizations of H.P.B.'s trance nature; or – just possibly – spirits; or else "the trance principle of nature expressing itself symbolically" '.)

Earlier, Annie had written that Theosophy conveyed 'no very definite idea of the requirements for membership, beyond a dreamy, emotional, scholarly interest in the religio-philosophic fancies of the past'. She *was* emotional, she was scholarly, she was dreamy, though she had forced these traits underground for a long time. Let the last word on her conversion come from Shaw, so long as it is taken with a kindly grain of salt:

She was a born actress. She was successively a Puseyite Evangelical, an Atheist Bible-smasher, a Darwinian secularist, a Fabian Socialist, a Strike Leader, and finally a Theosophist, exactly as Mrs Siddons was a Lady Macbeth, Lady Randolph, Beatrice, Rosalind, and Volumnia. She 'saw herself' as a priestess above all. That was how Theosophy held her to the end.

CHAPTER EIGHT

Certainly Annie liked to dress the part she was currently playing. Later, she was to wear black in mourning for H.P.B., with a small cross at her throat; later still, saris and robes. But when she joined the Theosophists she was still in her socialist outfit. Olcott noted

her air of a woman of the toiling class, with her thick, laced boots, her skirts somewhat shortened to keep them tidy when trudging through the muddy streets of the East End, her red neckerchief of the true Socialist tinge, and her close-cut hair – in short, an Annie Militant. Some of our people of the upper class in society were prepossessed against her, thinking that no great good could come from her importation of her fads and cranks into our respectable body. Some even protested to me against having her living at Headquarters, as it might keep influential women away.

Theosophy in England was snobbish as well as fashionable.

H.P.B., however, was under no illusion about the value of having acquired Annie Besant for her Society. Now fifty-seven (Annie was forty-two), she had been ailing and depressed for some time. Annie's conversion galvanized her into energy and happiness. When she wrote to her, Annie was 'Dearly Beloved' and 'My Darling Penelope' from 'Your

... female Ulysses'; 'I see your big lotus-eyes peeping into mine ...,' she wrote. Annie started to write and lecture for the Society straight away, and by the beginning of 1890 she was President of the Blavatsky Lodge, co-editor of *Lucifer*, and a member of the inner ring, the Esoteric Section.

Her former colleagues received the news of her conversion with dismay and in disarray. Bradlaugh, as Annie had expected, was deeply disillusioned. 'For thirteen years she had stood on the same platform with him,' wrote his daughter in her biography, 'and when one day she said that for ten years she had been dissatisfied with her own teaching, he felt it very keenly.' In the *Reformer* he wrote:

I very deeply regret that my colleague and co-worker has, with somewhat of a suddenness, and without any interchange of ideas with myself, adopted as facts matters which seem to me as unreal as it is possible for any fiction to be.

Shaw's reaction was less pained but more explosive. He, too, had been told nothing by Annie of her new direction. It was not until the summer of 1889 that he happened to see lying on a desk the proofs of an article headed '*Sic Itur ad Astra*; or, Why I Became a Theosophist'. Looking for the signature to the article on this fashionable topic, he saw to his astonishment and fury that it was signed Annie Besant.

Staggered by this unprepared blow, which meant to me the loss of a powerful colleague and of a friendship which had become part of my daily life, I rushed round to her office in Fleet Street, and there delivered myself of an unbounded denunciation of Theosophy in general, of female inconstancy, and in particular of H. P. Blavatsky.

Annie took the onslaught calmly. Shaw talked of the Society for Psychical Research's report, offered himself as a

left: Annie Wood at
sixteen
below: Annie Wood
with her mother

top: Annie Besant
bottom: Charles
Bradlaugh

→✳ Sabian Society, ✳←

MEETING AT ANDERTON'S HOTEL, FLEET STREET,

On Friday, 17th September, 1886, at 8 p.m.

Mrs. ANNIE BESANT

WILL DELIVER A LECTURE ON

✳"SOCIALISM AND POLITICAL ACTION,"✳

AND WILL PROPOSE THE FOLLOWING RESOLUTION:

"That it is advisable that Socialists should organise themselves as a political party, for the purpose of transferring into the hands of the whole working community full control over the soil and the means of production, as well as over the production and distribution of wealth."

ALL SOCIALISTS ARE INVITED TO BE PRESENT.

above: A card for a
Fabian lecture, 1886
left: Members of
the match-girls'
union, 1888

top: Madame Helena
Petrovna Blavatsky
bottom: Caricature
by Phil May

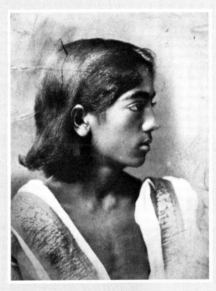

left: Krishnamurti in 1911
below: A group of leading Theosophists including Annie Besant, C. W. Leadbeater, Krishnamurti, Nitya

Annie Besant with daughter Mabel and grandchild

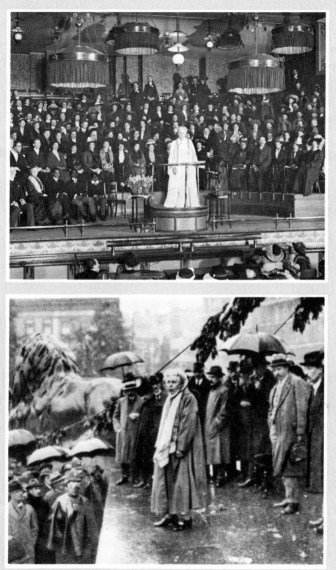

top: Annie at the Queen's Hall
bottom: Annie speaking in Trafalgar Square

above: Annie with Krishnamurti
left: In regalia, about 1925

better Mahatma than the Theosophists could offer, and generally did everything he could to tease and shame her out of her aberration. She just smiled and suggested that, since she had adopted vegetarianism like Shaw, perhaps it had enfeebled her brain. She was too confident, Shaw realized to his further astonishment, to rise to his teasing any more.

Over the next two years she was gradually to withdraw from her other commitments. For the *Reformer* she wrote another long piece on *The Secret Doctrine*, and Bradlaugh (unaware, no doubt, that Theosophists believed in life on Mars) replied that 'The "Masters" in Thibet are to me as the "inhabitants" of the planet Mars, and equally fall into the category of romance, whether vouched by Mme Blavatsky or by M. Jules Verne.' She was forced out of the National Secular Society; she left the Fabians; in 1891 she gave her last lecture at the Hall of Science. In the same year, she refused re-election to the London School Board. She withdrew from publication her birth-control book, incompatible as it was with her new belief that the evolved soul occupies itself with higher things.

She had not, though, dropped all interest in social improvement. For the Theosophical journal she wrote an article on 'Practical Work for Theosophists', emphasizing that they must show the world 'the sight of noble lives, strenuously and selflessly working for human good, battling against poverty and sorrow, the twin-daughters of Ignorance'. As part of this programme she oversaw the opening of a new Home for Working Women in the East End.

The publicity about her new allegiance made Theosophy even more the rage. Two very different men of letters were to drift in and out of it. Oscar Wilde's part was limited to attendance at parties; at a soirée celebrating the opening of a working girls' restaurant, attended by Annie Besant and a score of titled ladies, he had a lively discussion with H.P.B. on the relative merits of aestheticism and Theosophy. Perhaps he was picking up comic material.

W. B. Yeats was much more seriously interested in the occult; he had already come into contact with Theosophy in Dublin, and when H.P.B. settled in London he called on her – 'a sort of old Irish peasant woman with an air of humour and audacious power', he found her – and joined the Lodge. His assessment of her was that she was probably a genuine medium who was also given to romancing and trickery. G. K. Chesterton was to commend him for passing over 'their special spiritual prophetess, Mrs Besant, who was a dignified, ladylike, sincere, idealist egoist', and seeking out Blavatsky, 'a coarse, witty, vigorous, scandalous old scallywag'. The members who surrounded her Yeats dismissed as 'the usual amorphous material that gathers round all new things'. They turned every Theosophical doctrine into 'a new sanction for the puritanical convictions of their Victorian childhood,' he wrote. Like many others at the time, he had attended spiritualist séances which had impressed him, and he wanted to see what the Theosophists could come up with. His questioning attitude was not welcome, however, and he was asked to resign; a Theosophical lady had been found in tears after conversations with him. He moved on to continue his occult researches with the Hermetic Students of the Golden Dawn.

Annie herself was, she believed, having her first mystical experiences at this time. As she had not yet cut all her ties with secular work, she was attending a labour congress in Paris, and H.P.B. came over to complete some writings. After a day spent with her and other Theosophists, Annie went to bed and was awakened by the sight of a 'radiant astral Figure of the Master' in her bedroom.

She was to report many such meetings with astral guides throughout her life as a Theosophist; they appeared at convenient times and gave messages she wanted to hear. But it would go against all we know of her character to suspect her of simple lying. She had grown up in a family that took the supernatural for granted: 'belief in ghosts of all descriptions was general' in it, she wrote in her autobiography. Later, she learned from C. W. Leadbeater, her guide in matters occult, that whatever she saw in her imagination *was* a veridical vision; imagine a Master, and you have seen him. Her adopted son Krishnamurti was to say that when he was told of the god Krishna he 'saw' him, and when Theosophists told him of Koot Hoomi or the Lord Maitreya he just as easily 'saw' them.

Annie emphasized her commitment to Theosophy by offering her own house in St John's Wood for headquarters, as the Lansdowne Road house was too small for the growing movement. A building fund was set up and the house was adapted, with a suite for Madame, rooms for Annie and other members upstairs, and a new meeting hall, decorated with zodiacal symbols, built out into the garden. Above it were a number of bedrooms, so that the house could become a Theosophical community. Forbidden to all but the initiates was the Occult Room, furnished with mirrors and a glass ceiling, and said to be the scene of magical experiments.

To add to Annie's happiness, her two children, aged nineteen and twenty-one, were now voluntarily to join her. Digby, who scarcely knew her yet, had always intended to go to his mother when he was of age. He wrote to his father about his decision and received an angry letter back, cutting off all relations with him. Mabel had been secretly meeting her mother for some time; she, too, wrote to her father and received a similar reply. Poor Frank Besant, who seemed to have won all along the line, lost everything in the end. The young Besants, Annie wrote, were 'treading in my footsteps as regards their views of the nature and destiny of man, and have joined in their bright youth the Theosophical Society'.

Annie's time was now fully occupied with lectures, writing, and travel on behalf of the Society, as it had been before on behalf of Freethought and socialism. She was much occupied in expositions of Theosophy, in which she played down the cosmology and psychology and explained what it meant for her:

Theosophy is the body of truths which forms the basis of all religions, and which cannot be claimed as the exclusive possession of any. It offers a philosophy which renders life intelligible, and which demonstrates the justice and the love which guide evolution. It puts death in its rightful place as a recurring incident in an endless life, opening the gateway of a fuller and more radiant existence. It restores to the world the Science of the Spirit, teaching man to know the Spirit as himself, and the mind and body as his servants. It illuminates the Scriptures and doctrines of religions by unveiling their hidden meanings, and thus justifying them at the bar of intelligence, as they are ever justified in the eyes of intuition.

H.P.B. remained overjoyed by Annie's devotion; 'she is the most wonderful woman,' she wrote to her henchman in the United States, W. Q. Judge, 'my right hand, my successor when I will be forced to leave you, my sole hope in England as you are my sole hope in America'. But she understood the streak of literalness and humourlessness in Annie and warned Judge that when Annie visited the States there must be no irreverence about Theosophy and no deviation from the strict truth. She 'is the soul of honour and uncompromisingly truthful', she wrote, and 'filled to the brim with pure, unadulterated Theosophy and enthusiasm'.

Annie set out for the States in the spring of 1891. It was a year of deaths; Bradlaugh had died in January at the age of fifty-six, and H.P.B. was failing. The American tour was a great success, as were all Annie's speaking engagements. But when she docked on her return she was met with the news of Helena Blavatsky's death. Who was to succeed her? For months a power struggle rocked the Society. Olcott dithered about resigning; Judge was voted successor, then was demoted to being successor to the elderly Olcott. In the end Olcott remained President, with Annie Besant as head in Europe and India, and Judge as head in America. For all practical purposes Annie was now Theosophy's guiding spirit.

She had meanwhile caused a sensation which was to bring Theosophy even more into the public eye. Late in August she addressed an audience at the Hall of Science for the last time. The sensation came midway in her farewell address, and was reported thus by the newspapers.

You have known me in this hall for sixteen and a half years. (Cheers.) You have never known me to tell a lie to you. ('No, never', and loud cheers.) My worst public enemy has never cast a slur upon my integrity. ('Never', and cheers.) I tell you that since Mdme Blavatsky left I have had letters in the same handwriting as the letters which she received. (Sensation.) Unless you think dead persons can write, surely that is a remarkable feat. You are surprised; I do not ask you to believe me; but I tell you it is so.

The press exploded into argument, jokes and gossip. Most

of the material was sceptical and satiric – all the same, some papers pointed out, it *was* the famous Mrs Besant who was claiming to have had letters from invisible Masters. Correspondence columns were swamped with letters. One paper ran an article on 'How to Become a Mahatma'; the charge that Blavatsky had been a Russian spy was revived; a hatter designed a Mahatma hat, and it became the thing to ask 'How's your karma today?' Clergymen preached against the new religion, and the crowds at Annie's lectures grew ever more enormous.

She had planned to go to India for the first time that autumn, but was held back by the quarrels about the leadership. She made another successful visit to the United States. Finally, in the autumn of 1893, Annie Besant set out for India.

CHAPTER NINE

Annie docked first at Ceylon, where Olcott was eagerly awaiting her, already a hero to the Singalese because of the schools he had founded on the island (Olcott Street still faces the railway traveller alighting in Colombo). They were greeted with garlands and incense, and Annie's lectures were successful as ever. In mid November the party made the crossing to India and Olcott reverently noted the time Annie set foot on Indian soil – 10.24 a.m., at the village of Tuticorin. Their tour took them up and down India, through small villages and large cities; by Christmas they reached Madras, where Madame Blavatsky had acquired the splendid headquarters of the Society in the suburb of Adyar.

Annie was to make India her base for the rest of her life. Indeed she was to become so orientated towards Hinduism that letters appeared in the *Theosophist* protesting that the Society was committed to no specific religion. There was a different criticism from *The Times* itself: 'An English lady "spiritualist" is wooing Bengal audiences to her last new faith by assuring them that "if the youths of India would act up to the traditions of their past, instead of fawning on a foreign power, they would not long remain under a foreign yoke".' Annie, who had written on Indian problems as early as 1879, indignantly denied that she now touched on politics at all. For a surprisingly long time her work for India was to avoid politics.

She arrived back in England in the spring of 1894 to face a scandal that might have wrecked a lesser leader. She had made her great declaration that the Masters were still sending letters after H.P.B.'s death, and the English press had run riot. She had, indeed, seen letters on familiar paper, with familiar handwriting, apparently stamped with a well-known seal. Curiously, they were all concerned with the rectitude of Judge, leader of the American section and foe of Olcott: 'Judge leads right. Follow him and stick', 'Judge's plan is right', even a letter warning Annie that Olcott intended to poison her. Annie was, as H.P.B. had said, 'filled to the brim with pure, unadulterated Theosophy and enthusiasm' and – at first – did not doubt that they were genuine.

But even during her Indian trip evidence was accruing that she had been hoaxed by Judge over the letters. This was strong enough for her to manage a clinching astral visitation by the Master, telling her that Judge had forged them. Unadulterated enthusiasm was apparently not shaken – but Judge had to be dealt with. Councils and committees met, but it was for Annie to make the final decision about him, and this was the kind of task she had always found difficult. The woman who had shown such public courage was afraid, as she admitted in her autobiography, to take a firm stand with individuals:

When I have been lecturing and debating with no lack of spirit on the platform, I have preferred to go without what I wanted at the hotel rather than to ring and make the waiter fetch it . . . How often have I passed unhappy quarters of an hour screwing up my courage to find fault with some subordinate whom my duty compelled me to reprove, and how often have I jeered at myself for a fraud as the doughty platform combatant, when shrinking from blaming some lad or lass for doing their work badly!

So she made a roundabout speech explaining that she now realized that the letters had come only in spirit from the Master and had been actually written down by Judge. She had, she regretted, misled the public. And then she left for Australia, to spread the Theosophical word still further.

The ticklish affair seemed to have been quietly settled. But in fact the scandal was now to burst for the first time in the English press. While she was away a Theosophical 'mole' had leaked the matter to a freelance journalist, Edmund Garrett of the *Westminster Gazette*. Under the title of 'Isis Very Much Unveiled, Being the Story of the Great Mahatma Hoax', Garrett unfolded the story day by day for a fascinated readership; the haphazard founding of the Theosophical Society, the exposure by the Society for Psychical Research, the 'precipitated' letters from the Mahatmas, the scramble for leadership after Madame Blavatsky's death; the fact that the post-Blavatsky letters publicly described by Annie Besant proved to have been given her by Judge, stamped with a seal which Olcott once bought in a bazaar, on paper bought for book-packing. 'Ingenuous Mrs Besant!' indeed, as Garrett exclaimed.

Now just pause a moment, and enjoy the exquisite irony of this unique situation. The Theosophic Society was to be 'the nucleus of a Universal Brotherhood of Mankind'. At this moment, taking the three chief exponents of this new Brotherliness, the president believed the vice-president to be fabricating bogus documents; the vice-president apparently believed the president to have designs to poison the high-priestess; and the high-priestess, having these two beliefs to choose from, coquetted at least, as we have seen, with the more heinous of the two.

The fudging of the matter by Annie at the convention was made ruthlessly clear: 'I believe that Mr Judge wrote with his own hand, consciously or automatically I do not know, in the script adopted as that of the Master, messages which he received from the Master,' she had said; and Judge was declaring, 'I admit that I have received and delivered messages from the Mahatmas ... but as to how they were obtained or produced I cannot state.' But Judge was after all no forger, wrote Garrett, for

the verb, to forge, definitely connotes in English the imitation of the signature of a person who really exists, and who has also an existent banking account. The worst I should dream of imputing to Mr Judge in this connection is the imitation of someone else's imitation of the feigned signature of somebody who never existed.

And he concluded with a cruel cut at Annie: 'To this has come the woman whom we once thought, whatever her other faults, at least fearless and open – the woman whose epitaph, so she tells us, is to be – *She Sought to Follow Truth*!'

Correspondence poured in to the *Gazette*, from defensive Theosophists as well as an amused public. Judge published a pamphlet declaring that Annie Besant was the tool of black magicians. Garrett's articles and the succeeding correspondence were published as a book, with satiric verse appended:

> First I would remark that there must needs be painful scenes
> When Theosophic gents begin to give each other Beans;
> And though Mahatma missives do pan out a little queer,
> We should avoid disturbances in the Mahatmosphere.

Annie had committed herself up to the hilt to Theosophy, and could not afford now to doubt any part of it. If Master Koot Hoomi and Master Morya had *not* communicated since H.P.B.'s death; if therefore they had never existed outside H.P.B.'s imagination; if therefore *Isis Unveiled* and *The Secret Doctrine* had not been psychically transmitted to H.P.B. from them – then everything tottered. As she herself had written earlier, 'If there are no Mahatmas the Theosophical Society is an absurdity, and there is no use in keeping it up.' One might, perhaps, have expected the Society to have become a kind of secular social-work agency under her guidance, but in fact she was determined to take it ever deeper into the occult.

Meanwhile, she was conveniently in Australia and New Zealand while the storm raged in the press. On her return in the spring of 1895 it became clear that Theosophists were going to have to take sides for or against Judge. In the event the Irish branch, some English branches and a majority of the American branches set up a rival, pro-Judge group, but the parent Society survived and remained the stronger. For a decade there was to be peace, and Annie's literary output flourished on behalf of Theosophy, with a dozen books with titles like *Karma* and *Thought Power*, and innumerable pamphlets, coming out during that period. Olcott, in theory, reigned, but the old man was no more than a figurehead. Theosophy was now Annie Besant's kingdom.

But though she enjoyed power, particularly the power to sway audiences, she had never been egotistic enough to insist on ruling alone. She had always liked the support of colleagues, and there had usually been one especially influential one in each phase of her life. The man who was to come into her life now as prince consort of Theosophy was a less benign figure than Bradlaugh or Shaw.

Charles Webster Leadbeater can still, over fifty years after his death, arouse controversy. In occult circles some regard him as an unparalleled seer, others as a black magician, while the uncommitted may well see him as a figure of high comedy. What is more difficult is to explain him as an ordinary human being. It is, after all, difficult to call anyone ordinary who claims to have explored the planetary system in his astral body, seen the structure of the atom with his inner eye, been in frequent touch with the adept Masters of the earth, consulted the akashic records to describe the civilizations of Atlantis and Lemuria, talked to angels and archangels and found fairies in the water of Sydney Harbour which he sent by astral post to cheer the lonely. Yet Leadbeater was not psychotic, nor an absolutely straightforward fraud. It was a case again of tremendous lies told with tremendous panache, and dissociated from the everyday part of his personality. As a fantasist he was undoubtedly a phenomenon.

This is evident even in his account of his early life. By his own account, he was the son of a railway director, of aristocratic Norman stock. He went with his family to Brazil where, with his father and brother, he was captured and tortured by bandits. When his brother refused to desecrate a crucifix they killed him, and tied Charles himself to a tree and lit a fire under him. From this awkward situation he was saved by his brother's ghost and then by his father's timely arrival, and many spirited adventures followed, including a victorious hand-to-hand fight with the bandit leader.

In actual fact he was the only son of a book-keeper in Stockport, and never went near South America. He did not, as he claimed, ever go to Oxford, but was ordained into the Church and worked as a curate, living with his mother. He became interested in spiritualism, read Theosophical books, and at the age of twenty-nine was admitted to the Society, though there was some doubt about accepting a Church of England clergyman. He eagerly sent off a letter to the Master Koot Hoomi, and received a missive telling him to go and acquire skills in India. He duly spent five lonely years at Theosophical centres in India and Ceylon before coming back to join the London group, accompanied by several young boys whom he was tutoring.

During Madame Blavatsky's lifetime he remained obscure; she never liked him, and got some fun out of introducing him as W. C. rather than C. W. Leadbeater. Annie Besant was perhaps less of a judge of character. In the mid 1890s after Blavatsky's death, articles by him began to appear in Theosophical journals, and in 1895 he brought out *The Astral Plane: Its Scenes, Inhabitants and Phenomena* – the first of some eighty publications on reincarnation, clairvoyance, thought power, telepathy, spiritualism, the devachanic plane, dreams, angels, chakras, freemasonry, karma, the aura and vegetarianism. He was soon appointed to positions of some power within the organization, and began his partnership in clairvoyance with Annie. This is the period of her life with which it is hardest for modern readers to sympathize – and also a period when she seems to have been rather unhappy.

The chief joint venture of occultists Besant and Leadbeater was the investigation of previous incarnations of Theosophical worthies. It began with one of the members having a striking dream, which Leadbeater interpreted as coming from a past incarnation; Leadbeater then obligingly supplied him with a full history of his previous lives, from Chaldea in 2000 B.C., through Eskimo, Atlantean, Etrurian and other cultures. Much of his material was extemporized while sitting with other members on Sunday afternoons in a park at Wormwood Scrubs; a transcript shows that Annie contributed comments and questions and Leadbeater the gist of the stories. They went on to produce histories of all the leading Theosophists under pseudonyms; Olcott was 'Ulysses', Annie (most fittingly) 'Herakles'. Others investigated were 'Brihat' (Jesus Christ), 'Vajra' (Madame Blavatsky), 'Corona' (Julius Caesar), and 'Mercury' (the Master Koot Hoomi). Annie was honoured with fifty-three incarnations, among them a monkey (a very noble-minded one), a spirited Akkadian youth, a Buddhist missionary, a number of kings, queens and priests, and the martyr Hypatia. Much jealousy arose between those favoured with a reincarnation history and those left out. 'Oh, Mr Leadbeater, don't you think you could find me?' entreated a disappointed member, and Leadbeater promised to see what he could do.

Less voluminous but also wondrous strange are the books by Leadbeater and Besant on *Occult Chemistry* and *Thought-Forms*. In the former they analyse with the inner eye the structure of matter; the latter describes the physical auras of various emotions, and is illustrated with rather charming watercolours of them. An actor about to go on stage at a first night thinks in grey zigzags with an orange centre; the emotion of 'vague sympathy' is pale green and bulbous; a gambler who is losing ('observed at the great gambling-house at Monte Carlo') emits in his despair rings of black and scarlet.

There were also more mundane matters for Annie to attend to. The pro-Judge Theosophists in America, under the leadership of another determined woman, Mrs Katherine Tingley, were setting themselves up as the true heirs of Blavatsky. Mrs Tingley went to India and declared she had met the Master Koot Hoomi dressed as a Tibetan farmer; Mrs Besant went to New York ('Battle of Fair Sex Is On', said the headline) and fought Tingley with her highly successful colour slides of thought-forms. Both sides claimed victory.

Nor was Annie neglecting India, and her philanthropic interests. In Benares she founded the Central Hindu College, which was later to become a university. A number of other schools were opened over the years – one in Kashmir, a High School at Mandanapalle, a women's college in Benares. A Theosophical educational trust had to be established under her leadership to oversee all these projects. The young Jawaharlal Nehru himself was tutored by a Theosophist recommended by Annie, and has described his youthful enthusiasm for her and her teachings: 'I was twelve then and both her personality, the legends that already surrounded her heroic career, and her oratory overwhelmed me.'

Yet Annie seems not to have been particularly happy during these years. Her friend Esther Bright, one of the few people who saw the private Annie Besant, described her as lonely and tired. Before going on to the platform to give her usual dazzling performance she whispered to her, 'I am very miserable.' In the photographs of her as a young woman, it is the stubbornness of the mouth that strikes one; in old age she looks unassailable; but in her middle years there is a great deal of sadness in her face. She was a person who fended off doubt and depression by fighting, and perhaps there was not enough fighting for her at this time. She was committed to Theosophy, and could make no more lightning changes of allegiance. While she worked with Leadbeater on his 'researches' there may have been a good deal of doubt to fend off. He was now to cause her real heartache.

Leadbeater had always declared a special interest in education (of pubescent boys only), and was accustomed to travel around with two or three boys under his care. In 1906 the parents of one of these pupils brought serious charges against him. Their 14-year-old son had told them that Leadbeater had made him sleep in his bed at nights and had taught him to masturbate. Another couple, whose son had come out with a similar story, joined forces in accusing him. They declared, moreover, that rumours about Leadbeater had been rife for years and that Annie Besant had always turned a deaf ear to them. 'He made me promise not to tell,' said one of the boys; the other told his mother that the worst part of it for him had been that 'somehow he made me believe it was Theosophical'. Annie, unwilling as always to confront personal issues, fell back on defending Leadbeater. But damning evidence came from part of a coded letter addressed to 'My own darling boy' which, transcribed, read: 'Glad sensation is so pleasant. Thousand kisses darling.' Even Annie could not dodge this.

She managed, however, to be in India when a committee met to interrogate Leadbeater. Faced with his judges he seemed quite unruffled, but got himself deeper into the mire by admitting that he had shown his charges what to do ('indicative action' was the phrase) and had involved pre-pubertal boys. He had read their auras, he explained, and realized what their needs were. The committee demanded his resignation, and got it. Leadbeater wrote to Annie reminding her that he had been an ancient Greek in a recent incarnation. Annie was cool. He declared that she was under the influence of black magicians. Master Koot Hoomi dictated astral letters calling for his reinstatement. Annie continued aloof.

In fact their estrangement, unfortunately for posterity's view of Annie, was quite short; within a couple of years Leadbeater was a power in the Society again, undertaking more joint occult investigations. 'His only offence,' declared Annie, 'was that he gave a coterie of prematurely blasé young men some advice, which was exaggerated into a great fault and condemned as immoral teaching.' A number of influential members, however, resigned in protest. Their point of view was expressed by the head of the French section:

It is clearly manifest that Mrs Besant has fallen under the formidable suggestive power of her dangerous collaborator, and can only see, think, and act under his absolute control. The personality henceforward speaking through her is no more the author of *The Ancient Wisdom*, but the questionable visionary, the skilful master of suggestion, who no longer dares to show himself in London, Paris, or America, but in the obscurity of a summer-house at Adyar governs the Theosophical Society through its President.

For by the time this letter was written – summer, 1907 – Annie was at last President of the Theosophical Society. Olcott had died in February. As usual the Mahatmas had given their advice ('vote for Besant') while an opposing party of Theosophists had bandied about phrases like 'celestial Post Office' and 'inane and immoral babblings of the Adyar apparitions'. Annie's loyalty to Leadbeater had not helped her reputation. Nevertheless, when the balloting took place throughout the European, American, Australian and Indian groups, Annie Besant won by a solid majority. In the following year she celebrated with a barnstorming trip through Australia during which she estimated that she had covered 17,630 miles and held forty-four public lectures and ninety meetings – 'Not a bad record for a woman over sixty,' as she remarked.

CHAPTER TEN

The headquarters of the Theosophical Society at Adyar, Madras, is a green haven after the heat of the city, though today it has a touch of forlornness. The scattered buildings – Olcott School, Blavatsky Bungalow, Leadbeater Chambers – seem to be gazing back at the exciting early years of the century, and the huge marble hall with its statue of Madame Blavatsky dwarfs its frequenters. 'The vibrations here are wonderfully stimulating,' wrote Leadbeater during those years. The 250 acres of palms and casuarinas run down to the Adyar river; here in 1909 Leadbeater's attention was caught by two ragged Indian boys bathing with their friends. Krishnamurti and Nityananda Naryaniah were aged fourteen and eleven at the time, sons of an impoverished Brahmin Theosophist who had come to work at head-quarters. Their mother had died four years earlier and the children were dirty and neglected, Krishna a skinny little boy, sad, with a bad cough and lice in his hair. Nitya was brighter for his age, but it was the dreamy Krishna who had, said Leadbeater, the exceptional aura.

To understand the grooming of Krishnamurti for the role of successor to Christ, the place of a World Teacher in the Theosophical cosmology must be understood. Everything is forever evolving into more advanced forms and higher races, and is helped in its progress by great teachers such as Christ and the Buddha (Mahomet is less often mentioned). For some time before the choice fell on Krishnamurti, the theme of Annie Besant's lectures had been the coming of a new Avatar for the new sub-race. In fact a bright American boy was already being groomed for the part, but was dropped when it was felt that an Indian child had more mystique ('It is difficult for the American body to be as self-effacing and docile as the Indian,' wrote Annie).

Leadbeater plumped for Krishna – certainly a curiously prescient choice. By this time Leadbeater's astral trips and reincarnation researches were in full spate again. An Adyar resident has related how Leadbeater lay on the sofa one day to take an astral trip to Mars, and described streets, houses and inhabitants in great detail (not actually *material* streets, houses and inhabitants, the resident added). Annie relied on him to take care of everything on the further planes; to a woman enquiring about her deceased cat, he had written:

You need have no anxiety about the departed Tom. Your affection has brought him to the stage of individualization, and he will therefore not be reborn in feline form. You will therefore certainly encounter him in the course of evolution, but you must remember that it will be only at a much later stage, and therefore in another world than this.

It was natural therefore that Leadbeater should start Krishna's career by tracing his reincarnations and past relations with living Theosophists, under the name of 'Alcyone'. Adyar Theosophists soon caught on to the fact that Alcyone had been a key figure in past cycles, and besieged Leadbeater with queries about their previous connections with him.

Krishna did not have any obvious pretensions to his role, apart from a certain beauty. He was shy, spoke only Telugu, and was constantly beaten at school for stupidity. Leadbeater took over the two boys' schooling, and they were cleaned up, groomed and fed. By the time Annie returned from her summer lecture tour Leadbeater was able to present her with a personable future World Teacher, and as usual Annie was eager to agree with him.

The boys had already been taken (astrally) to meet the Master Koot Hoomi and prepare for initiation into the Great White Brotherhood. (Annie had become very keen on such organizations – Co-Masons, Lieutenants of the Lord, Order of the Rising Sun, Sons of India, Yellow Shawl Group, Temple of the Rosy Cross; members of the latter, both male and female, wore unisex white satin gowns with swords and headdresses and had the motto *Lux veritatis*, translated by one member as 'Looks very silly'.) Now Krishna, in trance, passed his initiatory examination and emerged as a consecrated vehicle; he held a meeting for his followers, the Order of the Star in the East, and they moved in a mass to throw themselves at his feet – 'white and dark alike, Brahmanas and Buddhists, Parsis and Christians, haughty Rajput Princes and gorgeously apparelled merchants, all prostrating themselves in rapt devotion at Alycone's feet', ran the account. At the same time, the initiate eye could see that

a great coronet of brilliant shimmering blue appeared a foot or so above the young head and from this descended funnel-wise bright streams of blue light till they touched the dark hair, entering and flooding the head. The Lord Maitreya was there embodying Himself in His Chosen. Within the coronet blazed the crimson of the symbol of the Master Jesus, the Rosy Cross, and high in the air well-nigh from the roof blazed down a dazzling flashing star which all initiates know.

Understandably, the Masters sent across a message that the new Messiah and his brother should now leave their father and move in permanently with the Theosophists; Narayaniah was persuaded to sign a statement giving Annie legal guardianship of them. She took them to her home in Benares first; and then, in the spring of 1911 as the hot season approached, the three set out for England – for the boys, their first trip away from home.

While Krishna and Nitya were being introduced to St Paul's Cathedral, performances of *Julius Caesar*, and Western shoes, Annie took part in the massive women's suffrage demonstration that was held in London that year, speaking with her usual success to an audience of ten thousand at the Albert Hall. She also lectured to Fabians, gave a talk in French in Paris, held debates with Christians and Moslems, and denounced vivisection and Indian child-marriage. Her final speech at the Queen's Hall was on the 'Coming of the World Teacher'.

When the party arrived back in India in the autumn they ran into a continuing anti-Theosophy campaign in the Indian newspapers. Though Annie Besant had adopted an Indian dress and way of life, and was respected for her work in education and her championship of all things Indian, her adopted land was showing signs of getting restive. The Indian papers seized on her two weakest points, the Leadbeater scandal and the adoption of 'the little Hindu boy she calls Alcyone'. The announcement of the coming Messiah was too much for some to swallow; the German Theosophists under Rudolf Steiner broke away and set up a separate organization, and a group of teachers at her Central Hindu College resigned in a body. At the same time, new members (perhaps not the most sensible and intelligent) were joining just because of the lure of the Messiah.

All this was not without its effect on Narayaniah, the boys' father. He demanded his sons back. For the moment Annie pacified him by sending Leadbeater abroad; but she went on to join Leadbeater in Taormina, a spot positively imbued with esoteric vibrations, where he had spent one of his previous incarnations as a magician. Here the Theosophical group consulted the akashic records and completed their massive record of past lives, *Man: Whence, How and Whither*. Then it was on to England to arrange a long spell of education and westernization for the two boys.

Narayaniah's acquiescence was only temporary. In the autumn he filed a suit for the recovery of his sons, citing several grounds: that Leadbeater had a scandalous reputation and was committing 'unnatural acts' with Krishna, that Krishna was being ridiculously deified, and that a book written by Leadbeater was being ascribed to Krishna even though he could hardly write a good letter in English. Annie denied all the charges, but rested her case chiefly on Narayaniah's unsuitability as a guardian. She also claimed that the case was backed by personal enmity towards her, both by the alternative group of Theosophists in America and by Indian extremists. It was beginning to acquire political implications because of the conflict of interest between the (mainly white and British) Theosophists and the Indian nationalists. As she had done before, Annie pleaded her own case in court, and counter-attacked by suing Indian newspapers for libel.

She lost the libel case, to her great indignation. When the case for allotting the boys' guardianship was heard in the spring of 1913, the question of Leadbeater's sexual interests became central. Both he and Annie denied all allegations. Nevertheless the judge's final ruling was that Narayaniah's sons should go back to him, chiefly on the grounds that Narayaniah could not have known that Krishna was to be groomed for the role of a new Christ. The newspapers, both Indian and English, broke into a flurry of comment, *The Times* declaring that Annie's undoubted influence over Indian youth was made dubious by her connection with Leadbeater.

Annie appealed; but the decision was upheld by the Appeal Court. In legal matters, however, she was a seasoned old campaigner, and she took the case on to the Privy Council in London. Early in 1914 the Lord Chancellor and a formidable array of English legal talent ruled that Annie Besant should have the guardianship of the Narayaniah boys – the determining factor being that the boys themselves wanted this. They had been housed and educated by the Society for some time, and to go back to the poverty and dirt of their family home was unthinkable. Leadbeater went off to Australia, where he set up a pseudo-Christian organization called the Liberal Catholic Church and had himself ordained bishop. Henceforward he appears in photographs in full regalia, a large pectoral cross resting below the Santa Claus beard.

Krishna and Nitya, now aged fifteen and nineteen, settled down in Britain to study throughout the years of the First World War, though Nitya managed to spend a few months in France as a despatch-rider. Krishna's attempt to enlist was vetoed by Annie on the curious grounds that in the

army he would have to eat meat. The story of Krishnamurti's life is an extraordinary one which can only be
touched on where it is part of Annie Besant's. In those years
of delayed adolescence he was restless and unhappy, failing
his university entrance examinations with monotonous
regularity. 'Why did they have to pick on me?' he often
asked.

CHAPTER ELEVEN

If Annie had started the training of the Saviour-to-be partly out of her addiction to new projects, the war now forced her to leave the undertaking, like a discarded toy, in England for the duration. With Leadbeater away, occult researches too could take a back seat – though in her new political work for India she was to keep to her habit of declaring her actions to be approved by invisible Masters.

When in 1894 she had made India her home and headquarters she was deep in her Theosophico-religious phase and forswore all involvement in politics. Her earnest belief, she declared, was that

the future of India, the greatness of India, and the happiness of her people, can never be secured by political methods, but only by the revival of her philosophy and religion. To this, therefore, I must give all my energies, and I must refuse to spread them over other fields.

For a long time she had kept this resolution. By its very existence the Theosophical movement had done much for Indian self-confidence; it had treated the colour bar with contempt and it encouraged Indians to respect their religious and literary heritage. 'She implanted the seeds of self-respect in this land of slaves of government and tradition,' wrote an

Indian colleague. Annie herself saw her work for India as divided into four phases: up to 1898, it was chiefly religious; from 1898 to 1903, educational; from 1903 to 1913, social; and from 1913 onwards, chiefly political. As early as 1902 she had in fact been writing that 'India is not ruled for the prospering of the people, but rather for the profit of her conquerors, and her sons are being treated as a conquered race'. She had encouraged Indian national consciousness, attacked caste and child-marriage, and worked effectively for Indian education. It was inevitable, with her restless need to build new empires, that she should move on to active political work. As she put it in the familiar Besantine 'thrilling voice': 'Liberty was being strangled to death, and I, as one of her old soldiers, could not stand aside. I joined the political campaign not to lead, but to take risks.' She did take risks, and she also led. And when she started her campaign she was sixty-six.

India's growing sense of national pride had produced some reforms and had established, in 1906, the first National Congress. Though the Congress at that date had no effective political power, it met once a year and was an important national symbol. At the same time the Swadeshi movement for economic independence, the use of home-made rather than imported goods, was gaining ground.

Within the Congress two factions had developed, the moderate and the extreme, and these were still in opposition when Annie Besant came on the political scene.

Her own accusations against British rule were that it had milked India of its natural wealth, stifled native industries, neglected education, agriculture and sanitation, kept Indians out of senior positions, and in general ruled the continent autocratically and selfishly, without respect for

Indian culture. The current talk of England being trustee for Indian welfare she dismissed as cant. During her remaining years she was to write some dozen books on these themes. She was not demanding independent statehood for India, but self-government under Britain, leading to colonial status. Her new stand, however, aroused a good deal of dissatisfaction among loyal British Theosophists. They were prepared to grant India the lead in ancient wisdom, but not political power.

Already, while the Krishna decision was pending, Annie had begun to bring the Society into the public eye by accepting invitations to the conventional world of state receptions and official garden-parties. Then in the autumn of 1913 she started a series of eight lectures with the challenging title of 'Wake Up, India'. In them she demanded an end to the petty animosities within India, the reform of child-marriage and the caste system, better rights for Indian women, and a revival of the *panchayat*, the self-governing village council. To spread her message further she started a weekly journal called the *Commonweal*, subtitled 'A Journal of National Reform'. It followed with particular interest the progress of Gandhi and his 'passive resisters' in South Africa and noted that he had spoken there of the debt he owed to the Theosophical Society – it had turned him towards spiritual things at a time when he was young and sceptical, he said. He and Annie Besant were not always to remain on such an amiable footing, however.

Inevitably, Annie received supernatural backing for her new ventures. Her astral voyage this time was not to Koot Hoomi but to India's special ruler, the Rishi Agastya, who dwelt invisibly with his king at Shamballah in the Gobi Desert. The message received was that she must 'Press steadily the preparation for the coming changes and claim India's place in the Empire. THE END WILL BE A GREAT TRIUMPH. Do not let it be stained by excesses. Remember that you represent in the outer world the Regent, who is my Agent. My hand will be over you and My Peace with you.'

While she was in London pursuing the ultimately successful fight for the guardianship of Krishna and Nitya she took the opportunity of writing to English newspapers, lecturing on India, and attending as many functions as she could to spread the word. During her stay she was able to show that she had not cut herself off from her socialist past. The Society was having labour problems with their new London headquarters; the building workers had gone on strike and had been locked out by their bosses. Annie asked that the workers and their union should negotiate directly with the Society and this was successfully done, to the great indignation of the middlemen.

When she got back to India she launched a second successful journalistic venture; she bought up a moribund Madras daily newspaper and reissued it as the *New India*, writing most of the editorials and many of the regular columns herself. All the other full-time staff members were Indian. The paper stood for self-government, an end to racial prejudice, and better living conditions for Indians. Within a few months it had doubled its circulation. Then in August 1914 the First World War broke out. *New India* immediately urged that the country should give all the aid it could to the Allies. Annie's personal explanation of the war was that Germany was under the control of the Black Powers. She by no means shelved her demand for self-government for the duration of the war, however, which made her highly unpopular in Britain but a heroine to the Indians.

By the beginning of 1916 Gandhi had returned to his native land after many years of struggle in South Africa, bringing with him the concept of passive resistance that had guided his campaigns so far. Annie admired him, but she doubted whether his method would make sense to the masses or bring him any political influence. Their disagreements were to grow fiercer with time. Nevertheless, in the *Commonweal* she described him as 'one of the earth's really great men' and reminded readers that she had first met him in 1889 at Madame Blavatsky's.

All the time she was continuing to work for and through the National Congress – speaking, writing a record of its history, and trying hard to reconcile the extreme wing with the moderates. Late in 1916 she set up the Home Rule League, attracting police attention and considerable hostility from the white press. Once again Mrs Annie Besant was becoming a serious annoyance to the Establishment.

Her first serious clash with Gandhi had come early in 1916, at the grand opening ceremony of the Hindu University, which had grown out of the Central Hindu College she founded. When Gandhi stood up to make his speech he launched straight away into an attack on the jewelled Indian princes sitting behind him on the platform. They were indignant – some of them had sold jewels to help finance the university – and they staged a walkout. Annie was horrified, and accused Gandhi of provocation; the meeting broke up in confusion. To her further annoyance, the Indian papers took Gandhi's side. In her own two papers she tried to redress the balance.

In spite of her policy of relative moderation, Annie was now being hounded by the police. Her mail was interfered with, her books were tabooed, and the *New India*, with several Indian newspapers, was threatened with closure under the Press Act. When an order for her externment from Bombay was passed (the grounds being that 'Mrs Annie Besant has acted and is about to act in a manner prejudicial to the public safety'), protests and petitions poured in. The Congress meanwhile had adopted the doctrine of Home Rule as their own, and Annie's name began to be mentioned as a future President.

There had been rumours for some time that she was to be interned until the end of the war. In the summer of 1917 the Governor of Madras called her to a private interview and offered her a safe conduct to England, which she indignantly refused. In that case, he said, she would have to be interned, but he would not give any specific reason.

I arose and he walked with me to the door, and on his way he said, 'I wish you to consider, Mrs Besant, that we cannot discriminate and the whole of your activities will be stopped.' I said, 'You have all the power and I am helpless, and you must do what you like. There is just one thing I should like to say to Your Excellency, and that is that I believe you are striking the deadliest blow against the British Empire in India.'

Annie was never at a loss for a resounding final word.

'What is my crime,' she asked in the *New India*, 'that after a long life of work for others, publicly and privately, I am to be dropped into the modern equivalent of the Middle Age *oubliette* – internment?' But the Governor was not to be swayed. A few days later, accompanied by two Theosophist colleagues, she left Madras for internment in Ootacamund, and was seen off at the station by huge crowds.

One might have expected that a rest from her labours in the pleasant hill climate would have been quite welcome to

Annie, at the age of nearly seventy. In fact this seems to have been the one time when she broke down completely. Work had been her drug, and now she was deprived of it. As the weeks of internment went by she grew continually weaker and more depressed. Nothing could have been further from the quietism of the Eastern religions incorporated into Theosophy than Annie's compulsively busy way of life; but now there was nowhere to go and nothing to do. Friends who visited her found her old and broken, eating little and sleeping little. All over the country, meetings of protest against the internment were being held, and photographs of the three prisoners sold for an anna apiece. 'Who would have thought there would have been such a fuss about one old woman?' asked a disgruntled government official.

Eventually a group of anxious colleagues turned to Gandhi for help. His suggestion was a pilgrimage of volunteers across the thousand miles between Bombay and Annie's bungalow, to arouse public concern; but the idea was turned down as impractical. It was in fact her influential Theosophist friends in England who brought pressure to bear on the government; and after ninety-four days of internment, still weak and ill, she was released. Indians everywhere were overjoyed; the British in India were glum.

The prospect of work to be done revived Annie in no time. She knew that her name was now being seriously brought forward as next President of the Congress; while she was still interned a number of provincial committees had chosen her as their candidate. Her popularity was at its height, and when she stepped out at Madras station the crowds stretched along the whole route to Adyar. Straight away she set out on a lecture tour through northern India, where she found the audiences and the excitement she had missed so sorely during her seclusion.

She was at the peak of her popularity in India now, a national heroine. When Montagu, the new Secretary of State for India, met her, he commented afterwards in his diary, 'If only the Government had kept this old woman on our side! If only she had been handled well from the beginning! If only her vanity had been appealed to!' The meeting with Montagu was just a prelude to the high point of all her work for India, her Presidency of its National Congress in December 1917.

It was the largest Congress ever yet held. A great amphitheatre to seat some 9,000 people was specially constructed; the procession that lined up for Annie's arrival was the biggest yet. Banners and garlands were hung above the route, bands played, flower petals showered down on her. To her whole varied career this was perhaps the climax – but it was to be an ironically short moment of triumph.

Her Congress speech was not quite the riveting success she was accustomed to, and *The Times* in London, always hostile to her, commented on the paradox of an elderly white lady being the one chosen to represent all India. From an opposed point of view, India was about to agree with *The Times*. From now on, as Gandhi's status rose, Annie Besant's started to decline. She had begun to fall between two stools – Indian nationalists found her outdated and too moderate, the English considered her wildly extreme. And she never quite reached the heart of the masses as Gandhi did; her greatest popularity had been among educated Indians, so much influenced by Theosophy.

The year after her Presidency of Congress, Montagu published his proposals for Indian reform; Annie declared them outrageously inadequate, as did the Indians themselves. Later, however, she was to suggest that with modifications they might be acceptable, and this was not forgiven her. Gandhi meanwhile was winning battles with his passive resistance policy, which Annie had always opposed, and her own Home Rule League rejected her as President in favour of Gandhi. One of her Indian followers has written of how horrified he was when an audience of students heckled and insulted her. 'All these forty years my white body has been an asset,' she said to him. 'It is no longer so, and the youth of India has become normal in its behaviour. My work has been crowned with success.' Yet she would scarcely have been human if she had not also been hurt.

In April 1919 an event occurred which was to put an end to the moderate influence in India and undo years of reformist work. At Amritsar in the Punjab, General Dyer opened fire without warning on an unarmed gathering of Indians, killing nearly 500 and wounding 1,200 more, whom he ordered to be left to die in the open. The ultimate brutality was that the British in India subscribed a fund of £30,000 for Dyer as a reward for his deed. Annie was entirely at one with the Indian public in her outraged reaction, but she could not resist reminding that public in her newspapers that she had predicted all along that Gandhian non-violence would lead to violence. After a summer spent in England preaching the Home Rule cause – the first since the war broke out – she returned to India to find herself, her moderation and her white skin all discredited. India was to award her an honorary doctorate in 1921, but it was no more than a gesture towards an old, discarded friend.

CHAPTER TWELVE

In the summer of 1920, when the first world congress of Theosophists was held in Paris, Annie was seventy-two and had forty-six years of public work behind her. India, after so many years, seemed to have rejected her, and she was free to give first place to Theosophical affairs. Fourteen hundred delegates from thirty-nine countries attended the gathering; if she had been superseded at home in India, she still had a Theosophical kingdom to rule over. Unfortunately it was a kingdom racked by feuds, rivalries, accusations and counter-accusations. The storm-centre, as before, was Leadbeater.

He had settled in Australia at the beginning of the war, but it was not long before he began to set up little kingdoms of his own there. Various youth organizations were set up for his young protégés – the Golden Chain, In the King's Service, the Order of the Round Table (in which he made himself Senior Knight-Founder Sir Lancelot). But these were not quite enough; with his usual unshakable aplomb he now took over a small Christian sect that called itself the Old Catholic Church, renamed it the Liberal Catholic Church, and had himself and several other Theosophists ordained bishops. Although there was already a special Krishnamurti organization, the Order of the Star in the East, the new group fitted in well with the plans for Krishnamurti's emergence as World Teacher; the Indian Christ would have a Church to lead, complete with vestments, liturgy and hierarchy. From India Annie had endorsed the scheme: 'It is likely to be the future church of Christendom when He comes,' she wrote. Of course in a way he *had* come; Krishnamurti certainly existed, but he himself was considered only a Vehicle for the World Teacher to inhabit. Privately many Theosophists were wondering if they had backed the wrong horse. When Annie had made her first post-war trip to see 'her' boys in England, the twenty-four-year-old Krishnamurti was still a bewildered young man whose only act of rebellion against his fate was to fail examinations.

The creation of the Liberal Catholic Church appalled many Theosophists in Australia and elsewhere; the American branches were especially hostile. In addition, Leadbeater's brother bishop Wedgwood and several other Liberal Catholic clergy were being pursued by the police with the same charges of paedophilia against them that Leadbeater had always managed to fend off. With her misguided sense of loyalty Annie did not sack the lot of them, but publicly came to their support in her Theosophical journals. The world congress of 1920 was a very divided house to rule over.

Young Krishnamurti, who was worried about tuberculosis in his beloved brother, heard of nothing but harmony and faith, badges and initiations and the astral plane, but in spite of all the brainwashing he had patiently undergone he was becoming more and more sceptical. Not surprisingly, the theme of his teachings in later life was the futility of authority, organizations and dogma. 'Heavens, how I hate it all,' he wrote from Australia to his Theosophical foster-mother, Lady Emily Lutyens:

> As I go about the street the people nudge each other & point me out; the other day one chap said to the other, 'There goes that chap printed in the papers, the Messiah!' Then they burst out laughing. I should have laughed too if I hadn't been there or involved in anyway . . . I shall have it all my life. Heavens, what have I done to deserve all this.

Nevertheless he was induced to stand up at a Theosophical gathering and declare Leadbeater the purest man he had ever met. Annie had come with the two young men to Australia to try to calm the storms; though she kept thirty-four public engagements in the twenty-four days she was there, she left them uncalmed. Some Theosophical sects broke away from the parent body. An Australian Theosophist whose young son was seduced by Leadbeater opined that Annie was not actually a liar but was 'a foolish, egotistical and misguided woman, who, even if she realized her mistake, was unwilling to retrace her steps'.

From astral Mahatmas she turned back to her problems with India's flesh-and-blood Mahatma, Mohandas Gandhi. Under his leadership, Congress had now voted to back his policy of non-cooperation; Annie publicly dissociated herself from this, declaring that it would lead to riots and bloodshed (as it did). 'The Parting of the Ways' was the title of her *New India* editorial at the beginning of 1921. But Gandhian policies were catching on in a way that Annie's middle-of-the-road proposals never had; so much so, in fact, that in 1922 Gandhi was charged with sedition and sentenced to six years' imprisonment, of which he was actually to serve only two. Annie took advantage of the lull to promote an idea that was temporarily to give her back some of her old influence. Her proposal was that Indian leaders should draft a constitution for their country and have it recognized by Parliament in London, as a further step on the road to self-government. Energetically she set wheels in motion, backing the movement up by a campaign in her newspapers.

The year 1925 was one of crisis for both her projects – the presentation of her young Messiah and of her work for a constitution. Both seemed to be headed for success. The previous year had been a reassuring one; in celebration of her fifty years of public service people had flocked to pay tribute to her, including her generous enemy Gandhi, who wired:

I wish to express my admiration for this long record of service and the amazing energy and courage that lay behind it. I cannot forget, though it is many years ago, the inspiration I drew from her in my boyhood and then again in my experiences of political activity.

A London magazine had commented that 'Gandhi's only rival in India is a woman – perhaps the most remarkable of living women'. She had every hope then that her Bill on the Indian constitution would be backed both in England and in India. In fact the Bill was presented to Parliament as a private member's measure, went through only one reading, and was indefinitely shelved.

On the Theosophical front, too, everything seemed at first to be going extraordinarily well in that year. At the Liberal Catholic headquarters and at the Star camp – supposedly held for Krishnamurti, but he was away nursing his sick brother – there were tremendous developments; members astrally passed their initiations, new priests and bishops were ordained by the Lord Maitreya, and the Masters sent through no end of instructions ranging from the wearing of silk underwear to the provision of twelve apostles for Krishnamurti. He himself, deeply worried about his now dying brother, was so disgusted by these developments that he later had his letters of that period destroyed, as they were so critical of Annie and her fellow members. Outwardly he continued to play his part, even speaking so movingly at the massed convention at Adyar that Annie decided that the World Teacher had indeed descended into his body. 'We knew,' she wrote, 'that the waiting period was over, and that the Morning Star had risen above the horizon, presaging the dawn of a new Day . . . We are at the beginning of a New Age, a new civilization.' But the young Messiah was storing up all these things – initiations, apostles, bishops, Masters – in his heart.

His talks were getting more and more unorthodox, to the exasperation of seasoned old occultists like Leadbeater. He talked of the futility of sects and dogmas, which Theosophists had relied on for so long, and of the need to think for oneself. 'There are going to be no miracles nor strange happenings,' he disturbingly declared. To the Masters, the foundation stone of the whole Theosophical enterprise, he made no reference at all. The Liberal Catholic Bishops took counsel, then spoke to Annie; Krishnamurti was obviously being possessed by a Black Magician, they advised, and it was her duty to tell him so. She did, and he offered to stop public speaking altogether. This would have been very awkward indeed and, deeply worried, she had to leave the dilemma unsolved. At the next gathering Krishnamurti caused consternation by joking that he had never been able to read through a Theosophical book in his life. Generously, he was to declare that 'What I am saying is for everyone, including the unfortunate Theosophists.'

He never lost his affection and respect for his adoptive mother Annie, though. In 1926, tacitly avoiding awkward topics, they spent some time together in California, where Annie bought a large property to accommodate future gatherings (after some havering over Australians, the Californians had been chosen as the evolving sub-race that Krishnamurti was to lead). They went on to England, and Annie took a group on a lightning tour of Europe to give fifty-six lectures. Everyone but herself was exhausted. Then it was back to India to celebrate her eightieth birthday, and a further round of talks and committee meetings. Her great treat was to dress up in a specially designed uniform and march at the head of 12,000 Indian Boy Scouts, back in 1916 she had founded the first Boy Scout organization for non-white boys.

It was in the summer of 1929 that the blow for which Krishnamurti had been preparing his audiences fell at last. He was now thirty-four and Annie Besant a failing, though still formidable, eighty-one. Leadbeater and his other Theosophist teachers were old men. Krishnamurti had reached the point where he could repudiate years of conditioning and show that he thought for himself and decided for himself. He stood up before 3,000 disciples at the Star camp and formally disowned Theosophy and the Order of the Star.

'You are accustomed to authority', he told them;

For eighteen years you have organized, you have looked for someone who would give a new delight to your hearts and minds, who would transform your whole life, who would give you a new understanding; for someone who could raise you to a new plane of life, who would give you a new encouragement, who would set you free – and now look what is happening! Consider, reason with yourselves, and discover in what way that belief has made you different – not with the superficial difference of the wearing of a badge, which is trivial, absurd ... In what way are you freer, greater, more dangerous to every Society which is based on the false and the unessential? In what way have the members of this organization of the Star become different? ... You are all depending for your spirituality on someone else, for your happiness on someone else, for your enlightenment on someone else.

Detached now from the Theosophical Society, Krishnamurti was to continue to preach his quietist message of honesty and acceptance (he died only months before the publication of this book). Privately the dyed-in-the-wool Theosophists fumed over him – 'the Coming has gone wrong,' said Leadbeater – but publicly things were smoothed over under Annie Besant's leadership.

And she, it began to seem, was defying the law of mortality. She still travelled, she still wrote, she still lectured. But gradually she grew frailer and more forgetful, gradually her speeches grew shorter. The *New India* was closed down. She wanted to resign from the Presidency of the Society, she declared, but a message from the Master had forbidden her to. And she would return in a Hindu body in her next life to continue her work for India. When Krishnamurti visited her in 1932 he wrote: 'It was really tragic. Her voice had changed like an old, old woman's, very thin. She recognized me. She said to me, "I am so glad to see you" (two or three times she repeated) "you look so well. I brought you up, didn't I?"'

In September 1933, just before her eighty-sixth birthday,

121

Annie Besant died peacefully. Telegrams and letters poured in, the press printed tributes, the Stock Exchange in Bombay closed for a day and the Hindu University closed down its classrooms. Streets were renamed for her and in Madras a little park was laid out and a statue of her set up.

Annie Besant presents a challenge to our empathy and understanding today. It would be easy to stress only the parts of her career that appeal to us – her feminism, her anti-racism, her struggle for the underdog – and gloss over what we find irrelevant or absurd. But we *must* take her as a whole, rooted as she was in Victorian religiosity as in Victorian public-spiritedness.

Debunking comes easily enough; of course the life of public service was also a life enabling her to listen to the sound of her own voice a great deal and to organize the lives of others a great deal – activities which she decidedly enjoyed. We are disillusioned enough now to know that nobility and self-sacrifice have their private, selfish sides. She worked ferociously hard – but it was because she had to, because she was fundamentally not a happy person, because work was her preferred drug. Ironically, the most telling criticism of her way of life comes from her adopted son Krishnamurti, who loved and admired her:

If we had no belief, what would happen to us? Shouldn't we be very frightened of what might happen to us? If we had no pattern of action, based on a belief – either in God, or in communism, or in socialism, or in imperialism, or in some kind of religious formula, some dogma in which we are conditioned – we should feel utterly lost, shouldn't we? And is not this acceptance of a belief the covering up of that fear – the fear of being really nothing, of being really empty?

Annie Besant's failings were inextricable from her qualities. She was a deeply loyal person, but this meant that she turned a blind eye to faults once her loyalty was given. She had extraordinary powers of concentration, a kind of tunnel vision regarding the enthusiasm of the moment which enabled her to focus all her energy on it; but this meant a compartmentalism, by which she shut out and denied everything else. She was not vain in any petty sense, but her loyalty and single-mindedness went with a very great dislike of admitting herself wrong. And, having taught herself to believe in the visions of her fantasy world, she formed the lazy habit of inventing a supernatural sanction for everything she decided to do.

On the credit side was, of course, her astonishing capacity for work, her administrative genius and her sheer guts. But to end there is not enough. These are not the qualities for which people are loved, and she was loved. She had a natural motherliness, and young Indians unselfconsciously called her 'Mother'. She could draw up a constitution for a continent, but she was also good at sitting up all night by sickbeds. She neither patronized nor toadied, whether she was in a slum or a palace. She had no talent for hating; she talked beautifully; she never blamed or whined or expected gratitude. 'A great woman, a strong woman ... a person we cannot forget easily,' wrote an Indian colleague on her centenary. It is time to remind ourselves again.

SELECTED BIBLIOGRAPHY

By Annie Besant

Annie Besant: An Autobiography. London: T. Fisher Unwin, 1893.
There is no complete bibliography of Annie Besant's writings. Geoffrey West (see below) lists seventy-five titles.

About Annie Besant

The Annie Besant Centenary Book. 1847–1947. Adyar: The Besant Centenary Celebrations Committee, 1947.

Besterman, Theodore. *Mrs Annie Besant: A Modern Prophet*. London: Kegan Paul, Trench, Trubner & Co., 1934.

Manvell, Roger. *The Trial of Annie Besant and Charles Bradlaugh*. London: Elek/Pemberton, 1976.

Nethercot, Arthur H. *The First Five Lives of Annie Besant*. London: Rupert Hart-Davis, 1961.

— *The Last Four Lives of Annie Besant*. London: Rupert Hart-Davis, 1963.

West, Geoffrey. *The Life of Annie Besant*. London: Gerald Howe, 1929.

Further reading

Blavatsky, H. P. *Isis Unveiled*. New York: J. W. Bouton, 1882.

— *The Secret Doctrine*. London: The Theosophical Publishing House, 1893.

Lutyens, Lady Emily. *Candles in the Sun*. London: Rupert Hart-Davis, 1957.

Lutyens, Mary. *Krishnamurti: The Years of Awakening*. London: John Murray, 1975.

Meade, Marion. *Madame Blavatsky: The Woman Behind the Myth*. New York: Putnams, 1980.

Price, Leslie. *Madame Blavatsky Unveiled?* London: Theosophical History Centre, 1986.

Tillett, Gregory. *The Elder Brother: A Biography of Charles Webster Leadbeater*. London: Routledge & Kegan Paul, 1982.

INDEX

INDEX